RICH'S DILEMMA

M. LEE PRESCOTT

Rich's Dilemma

by

M. Lee Prescott
Published by Mt. Hope Press
Copyright 2020, M. Lee Prescott
ISBN: 978-1-7330217-5-3
Cover design by Ashley Lopez
Cover images from Istock.com/ArthurHidden and haveseen/Bigstock.com

http://www.mleeprescott.com/

This book is a work of fiction. Names, characters, places, and events are products of the author's imagination or are used fictitiously. Any resemblance to actual people (alive or deceased), locales, or events is entirely coincidental.

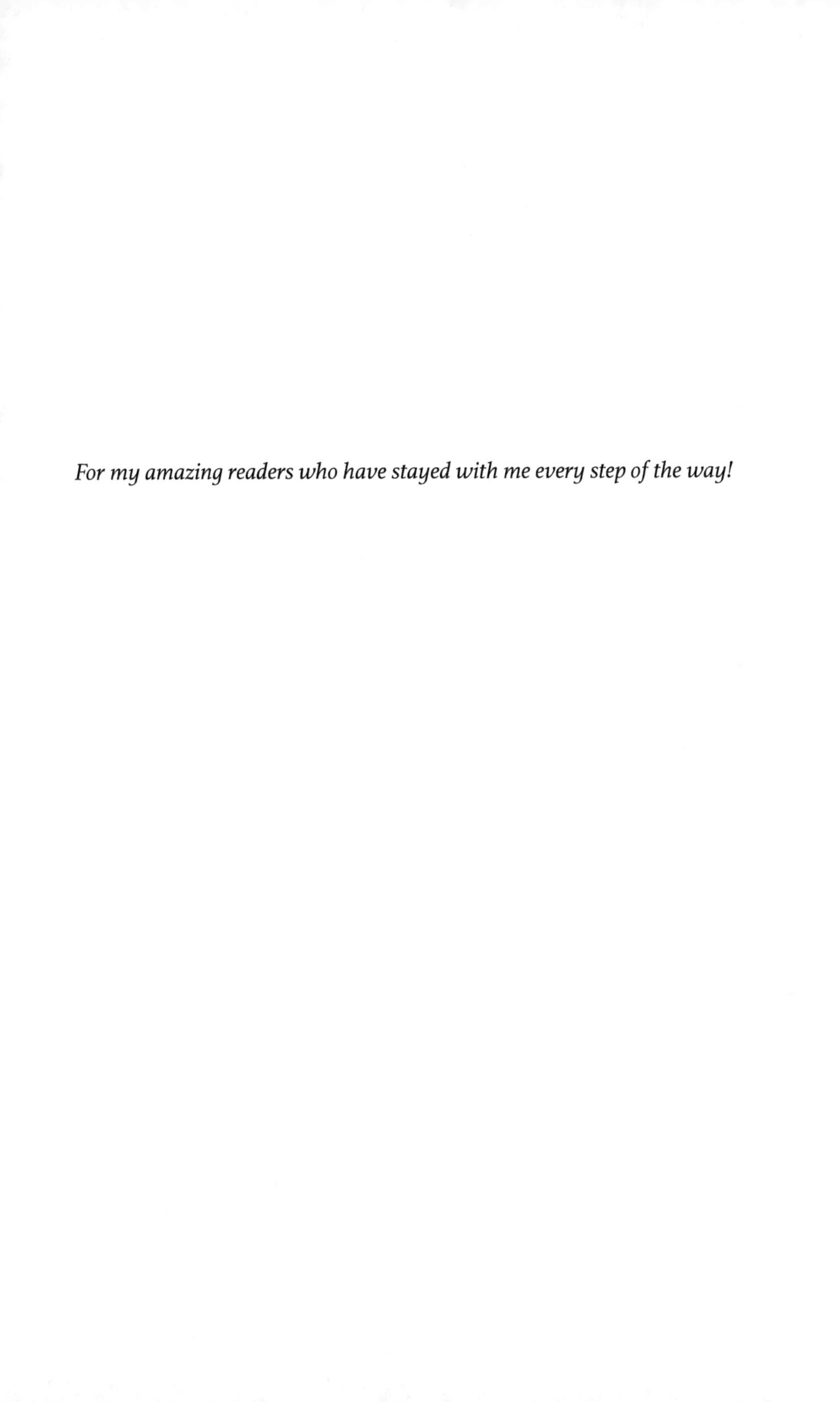

For my amazing readers who have stayed with me every step of the way!

CHAPTER 1

"We've caught it early, Rich. It's very treatable," Dr. Carina, the urologist, said. "I'm waiting for one more test, but I'm reasonably certain it will mean removal of your left testicle. That should be it unless the last test reveals lymph node involvement. The oncologist and I prefer to avoid chemotherapy and radiation unless absolutely necessary. We'll know better post-surgery."

Stunned, Rich Morgan stared at the short physician who bore an uncanny resemblance to Woody Allen. "When?" was all he could manage.

"The sooner the better. I'd like to schedule you for pre-op at end of this week and the surgery sometime next week. I'm at the Surgical Center on Tuesdays and Thursdays. The orchiectomy takes about thirty minutes to an hour. You'll need someone to drive you."

Rich sat silent, staring out the window for several minutes.

"You're going to be fine. It's very early stage, and the long-term prognosis for this type of cancer is one of the better ones."

"What about kids?"

"Are you planning to have one soon?"

Rich shook his head. "There's no one in my life right now, but I hope someday."

Dr. Carina smiled, placing a hand on Rich's knee. "Well, that's something to look forward to. This normally does not affect men's fertility."

"Okay, then. I guess I'm in. Is the recovery long? Will I need to take much time off from work?"

"I usually tell patients to take it easy for two to four weeks. No high-intensity exercise, but walking's fine after the first week. As for working, as long as it's not overly stressful or physically taxing, you should be okay to resume your normal schedule in three to four weeks. Important not to overdo. No heavy lifting and so forth. Should you find someone in the next few weeks, I'd advise against sexual intercourse for at least four to six weeks."

Rich gave him a wan smile. "Okay."

"Let me get Betsy in. She does all my scheduling." Dr. Carina slipped out, leaving Rich alone.

Rich stared out the window again. *Cancer. What will the family say? Should I even tell them? Of course I should.* Even though he seldom asked for it, he needed their support and love right now.

"Here we go," the doctor said, returning with his forty-something receptionist dressed in khakis, white blouse, and sage-green sweater vest, her long brown hair in pigtails. "Betsy, what have we got next week?"

After several minutes of conversation, they decided upon the following Wednesday at eight thirty in the morning. Betsy gave him several sheets of instructions. "I'll need to call over to the Surgery Center to get you a pre-op time. Is there a good day or time for you this week?"

"Any time's fine," he said, then thanked her and folded the sheets of paper in half.

"Okay then, I'll see *you* next Wednesday," Dr. Carina said. "If you have any questions before then, please call me. Cell number's on the information sheet."

Rich's mind raced as he exited the medical building and ran straight into Karen Miller. The armful of folders in her arms went flying, and papers scattered everywhere. "Oh gee, so sorry," he said, stooping to help her collect the papers.

"My fault," she said. "I was a million miles away."

Join the club, Rich thought, smiling at her. He hadn't seen Karen since her brother Tim's marriage to his sister Gail and thus had not acted on his fierce attraction to her. He couldn't exactly explain why. There was her love-'em-and-leave-'em reputation. There was also the fact that she was a spitfire and he was quiet, shy, and boring. Lapis-blue eyes met his as she brushed strands of curly brown hair from her forehead. She was barely five-four, so he towered over her.

"So was I. Can I help you get these back in the proper order?"

She winked. "No, I'll deliver them like this. Let them sort it out."

"Do you work here?"

She flashed a radiant smile. "Nope, I work two days a week for Andy Roby, the CPA."

"A numbers person."

Karen laughed. "Hardly. I'm a lowly receptionist and courier. How are you anyway? I haven't seen you since...?"

"The wedding."

"Yes, the wedding. Are you okay? You look a little pale."

"Just had some unsettling news. I'm heading home to digest it. Again, sorry about the collision."

"No worries. Listen, I'm just gonna drop these inside. Wanna grab a drink or even lunch?"

Rich was about to say no, but instead heard himself say, "Sure. I'll wait out here."

When Karen emerged from Cove Medical, she spied him sitting on a bench in the shade. He looked as though he'd lost his best friend. Even in dejection, the man was gorgeous. Long and lean with that straight sandy hair that was always falling in his face. Several times, she'd had to fight the urge to brush it back with her fingers. Then there were his father's bushy dark eyebrows that seemed out of place on the son's otherwise perfect face. The eyebrows were sexy as hell, but they belonged on a mischievous Irishman, not the quiet CEO of Morgan Enterprises.

"Hey, you ready?" she asked, startling him.

Rich jumped up. "I am. Where would you like to go?"

"Let's get sandwiches at the Café and walk down to your sister's garden. There are lots of shady spots there."

Rich nodded, brushing hair from his eyes. "Good idea, but she wouldn't want you calling it her garden." They referred to the community garden started by his younger sister Pam, just a short walk from the center of town.

Karen grinned. "I'll remember."

The Café was packed. As they made their way to the counter to order, Rich spied two of his sisters eating with Lynn Casey, wife of Gus Casey, their farm manager. He waved but continued to follow Karen toward the takeout counter.

"Hey, there's Pam and Gail," she said. "Just tell me what you want and go say hello if you want."

He didn't want, but felt awkward saying it. He handed Karen two twenty dollar bills, ordered a BLT, then headed across the crowded restaurant.

"Hi, ladies," he said, gazing around the table.

"Hello yourself," Gail said, grinning. "Hot date?"

"Hardly. Hi, Lynn, how are you and the family?"

"Great."

"Dad says you're all moved in. "

When Richard Morgan had lured the horse trainer east, he had written into Gus's contract the rights to a four-acre buildable lot on Morgan's Fire land. The farm was over five hundred acres, including several ponds, a vineyard, and prime waterfront property. It had taken nearly two years, but the Caseys' new home on Long Pond was finally ready for occupancy.

"Thanks to your dad's incredible generosity. It's a beautiful spot, and we're going to love it. The kids are in heaven."

Rich smiled. "It'll be great to have you out there."

Lynn looked up at him. "What about you? Think you might move out and build someday?"

"Someday maybe. Town suits me for now."

Pam stared at her brother. "You okay? You look a little green around the gills."

He nodded. "Fine. Better get going. Enjoy your lunch."

As he headed to where Karen stood, Pam turned to Gail. "Did he seem off to you?"

Gail shrugged. "Hard to tell with Rich. You know he's Mr. Calm, Cool, and Collected. No emotion, no drama."

"That's just it. He didn't seem calm, cool, or collected."

Gail smiled. "Maybe he's distracted by his date with Karen?"

"Maybe," Pam said, shrugging.

CHAPTER 2

They sat on a teak bench under an enormous maple at the far edge of Laura's Community Garden, named after his mother, Laura Morgan. There were a few gardeners and several volunteers working at various spots. The creation of the garden the past spring had been a community effort spearheaded by Pam Morgan and supported by many. Now in midsummer, all twenty of the raised beds were bursting with blooms—flowers, vegetables, herbs and fruit, each gardener's unique vision evident in the arrangement and choice of plants. After five minutes of silence, Karen turned to him. "How's your sandwich?"

"Can't ruin a BLT," he replied. "Especially on the Josie's sourdough." Josie Connors owned and operated the Crab Café with her husband, Paul. Josie was the baker, and Paul manned the grill. Most locals called it the Café, but it had been named for the region's beloved horseshoe crabs.

Karen nodded, taking a bite of her chicken salad on a warm baguette. "So how do you like village life? Must seem pretty tame after living all over the world."

"I was twelve when we moved back to the States. Our life in Maine wasn't all that different from here."

"Still, you've had all those cool experiences. I've never been anywhere."

He smiled at her, thinking she had the cutest turned-up nose. "Would you like to travel?"

"Would I? Not sure how that will ever happen. I'll probably be stuck here in Hicksville forever."

"You're not happy in Horseshoe Crab Cove?"

She shrugged. "It's my home. Of course I love it. It's just confining sometimes, you know?"

"Small town, big family, 'everybody knows your business' confining?"

"Something like that. How about you? Do you plan to stay?"

"For now, yes. My work is here. I lived in the city after college and didn't like it much. I mean, I love the theater and culture, but not the crowds. Everything and everyone moves so fast."

"How come a handsome guy like you isn't with someone?"

He grinned at the abrupt change of subject. "I had a girlfriend, but we've kind of petered out."

"Sara Gregson?"

Surprised, he said, "Yes."

She cocked her head, smiling. "Small town. Sara's a great yoga teacher."

"Yes, she is."

"So are you feeling better?" Karen asked, her blue eyes peering into his.

"Yes. Thanks for this welcome distraction." He shook his head. "Sorry, that didn't sound right, did it? I mean... I don't think you're a distraction. It was great to run into you. I have a lot on my mind, so it's good to have a respite for a while."

"Sometimes it helps to talk about it."

Rich hesitated. A very private person, he rarely shared anything with anyone. This had been one of the reasons for his breakup with Sara. Finally, he said, "As I said, I've had some unsettling news."

Karen met his eyes, but said nothing.

"I have cancer. I need surgery. Soon."

"Oh no, I'm sorry. Is it early and treatable, I hope?"

"Yes and yes. Or at least that's what they tell me. Just a shock, you know?"

For an instant, Karen spied the fear in his beautiful hazel eyes, but just as quickly, it was gone. "Of course it is. Is there anything I can do?"

"Have dinner with me sometime? Not sure if you have a boyfriend, so it could just be a friendly meal."

"I'd love to, and I don't have a boyfriend." She suppressed the urge to throw her arms around him and whisper that everything would be all right. She wondered about the cancer, but didn't think she should pry further.

"Great! I mean about your willingness to have dinner. The no-boyfriend too. Sorry, that made no sense."

Karen laughed. "I think I got it."

"This has been great. I'm sorry, but I've got to get going. I have a meeting at the vineyard in twenty minutes."

"Of course. I've got to get back to the office too."

They exchanged cell phone numbers then stood and walked out of the garden, waving to several of the gardeners. After stepping through the gate, she pointed to the house across the street. "This is me."

"That's convenient," he said. "I didn't know you worked in the same building as Pam." His sister and another therapist, Elise Nolan, had recently moved into the renovated Victorian, where they shared office and consulting space.

"Yup, but as I said, I'm only here part-time. Our paths rarely cross."

"Enjoy the rest of your day, and I'll be in touch about dinner," he said.

Karen nodded, then stepped forward to hug him. "I'm sure everything will be okay."

Startled, he returned her hug, wishing he could spend the rest of the day in her arms. After a few seconds, he released her and stepped back. "Thanks, Karen. Take care."

As Rich watched her walk into her building, he was aware that, despite the cancer, his libido was doing just fine. *Karen Miller is hot, and she smells great too,* he thought, the scent of citrus and spices lingering in her wake. *Not sure where the cancer will take me, but she is certainly something to live for!*

CHAPTER 3

"Hey, bro. We were about to give up on you," Wolfie Morgan said as Rich hurried into the winery's tasting room.

The youngest and oldest Morgan siblings were polar opposites. Where Rich was slender, fair, and preppy, Wolfie looked as if he'd just stepped out of the wilderness, with his long dark hair, thick beard, and coal-black eyes. Today, cleaned up in a blue button-down shirt and khakis, his hair in a ponytail, he looked every bit the part of a drop-dead-gorgeous vineyard manager.

To Wolfie's right at the table, a gray-haired, barrel-chested man nodded hello. The vintner, Zeke Ravensbrook's dark piercing dark eyes always sparkled with mischief. Across from Zeke, his assistant and apprentice, Cara Feldspar, leaned back in her chair. Her dirty-blonde hair in one long braid, she wore jeans, a flannel shirt, and work boots. Beside Cara sat a tan, blond stranger. Despite many Botox injections and what appeared to be extensive plastic surgery, Rich guessed him to be in his sixties, maybe older.

Wolfie gestured to their guest. "This is Gerald Manning. He owns—"

"Manning's on the Charles," Rich said, stepping forward, extending his hand. "Hello, welcome to Morgan's Fire."

Manning rose slightly and gave him a dead-fish handshake. "Thanks. It's quite a place you have here."

"Sit, please," Wolfie said, indicating the seat at the head of the table. "As I was saying, I manage the vineyard, but Rich here is the big cheese. He's the CEO of Morgan Enterprises."

Manning raised an eyebrow. "I thought the big cheese was the legendary Richard Morgan?"

As Rich smiled, exchanging looks with his brother, Wolfie said, "Not anymore. Dad's stepped down. He likes to keep up, but Rich is the man now."

"My father is a very skilled delegator," Rich said. "He's put people in leadership positions throughout his companies, and he trusts them."

"Lucky him," the restaurateur replied. "Can't trust anyone in my business. Employees rob you blind, and then there are the customers."

Rich decided not to pursue this line of conversation. "So, Mr. Manning."

"Gerry, please."

"Gerry, we're glad you're here and interested in partnering with Morgan's Fire."

"I pride myself on finding the newest and brightest stars in the food and wine business so I'm counting on you and these hotshot vintners to deliver me some spectacular wines." He directed these remarks to Cara, who opened her mouth as if to speak, but said nothing.

"Zeke is a genius," Wolfie said, endeavoring to redirect Manning's attention.

Manning nodded. "Of course he is. What do you think, Ravensbrook? Can you do it?"

Zeke shrugged. "The newest plants went in two years ago, so maybe a year for those. Might take two. Hard to tell. The old vines are doing well. We've nurtured the heck out of them, and we've had pretty good success bringing them back. Should know better in the fall, but we might get a small harvest."

Manning raised an eyebrow. "From what I hear, you're something of a miracle worker."

Zeke guffawed. "Hardly."

Wolfie spread a large map across the table. "As we said earlier, there are eight acres of old growth. That's what we've brought back to life. They're a gamble, but the twenty acres of new vines are coming along great."

"But you can't really say anything with certainty, can you?" Manning said, gazing from Zeke to Wolfie.

Wolfie paused, glancing over at his brother.

"Nope," Rich replied in a quiet voice. "That's why we invited you down to see the operation. Wolfie's probably gone over the varieties of wine we hope to offer you. We can, of course, buy grapes from other vineyards, but we hope to make our name with our own. Due to limited production projections, we're only reaching out to a few businesses for the first few years. You're one of them. You interested?"

His brother stared at him. It wasn't like Rich to be gruff or short. *Does he want to lose the account?* Manning's on the Charles was one of Boston's premier restaurants, written up in every wine and food guide in the world. "What my brother means is—"

"Shit or get off the pot, right?" Manning turned to Cara. "Sorry for my crudeness, doll."

Cara shrugged and directed her attention toward the head of the table.

Rich grinned. "Something like that."

"I'm in. Send me the projections and keep me updated. I'm willing to contribute seed money now, or even invest."

Rich waved his hand. "Thanks, but we're good. Our attorney will send a contract next week. At this stage, we don't need investors."

They spent another thirty minutes discussing things as they strolled the grounds. Finally, Manning departed with a wave of his hand as he slipped into his cherry-red convertible.

As the brothers watched the car disappear in a cloud of dust, Rich said, "We really have to do something about the driveway."

"Why? You afraid Gerry's Mercedes will get stuck in the mud?"

Rich grinned. "I couldn't care less if Mr. I Pride Myself drives off a cliff. It's just that the road's gonna take a beating once we have trucks and customers in and out. I vote for asphalt, but I know Dad'll veto that. I'll have Gail research more bucolic alternatives."

"Think Acadia," Wolfie said, slapping his brother's back as they headed for the barn. "Hey, you okay, Rich? You look kinda gray, and it's not like you to act pissy with clients."

Rich stopped near the barn door, taking a deep breath. "I've got testicular cancer. They're cutting off one of my balls next week."

"What? Jesus, man. How long have you known?"

"Since this morning. Haven't told anyone. I'll say something to Dad tonight."

"That's a bitch, man."

"Apparently they caught it early, so the prognosis is good."

"Sure it is. What can I do?"

"Nothing. I'm good. Maybe be there for dinner tonight?"

"You got it."

"Listen, Wolf, if it's okay with you, I'm gonna take off. See you later, okay?"

"Absolutely. We're good here." His brother gave him a bear hug.

"Thanks," Rich said, drawing warmth and strength from the embrace. He decided to head back to town to run a few errands and shower before the family dinner.

CHAPTER 4

"Our wine label is launched thanks to two of my brilliant offspring," Richard Morgan said, raising his glass as he gazed from Rich to Wolfie before his eyes settled on his second wife, Lucy.

Lucy smiled at him, love shining in her eyes. "Three of your brilliant offspring," she said. "Don't forget all Gail's PR work."

"You are right as always, my love."

Joining them for dinner were Amy, Lucy's daughter, Rich, and Wolfie. Weezie, the youngest Morgan sibling, was there, as were Richard's oldest daughter, Ava, and her husband, Dan. Dan and Ava's three kids were in the kitchen with Callie Richardson, cook and housekeeper. Along with their nanny, Marta Alves, Callie had them lined up at the counter, eating pizzas they'd made themselves.

Weezie still lived in the big house with Amy, Lucy, and Richard. Wolfie lived a mile away on the vineyard property. Rich lived in town, as did Richard's other children, Gail and Pam. Rob Brennan, Amy's brother, was working on the vineyard for the summer. Most Sunday nights, the entire family gathered at the long table, but this was midweek, when Dan and Ava often stopped by. Morgan's Fire had an "open table policy" where anyone was welcome any night. Somehow, Callie always had enough food on hand to feed four to twenty diners.

"Not quite launched," Wolfie said. "One potential sale."

"Manning's on the Charles, not too shabby," Dan Fielding, his brother-in-law, said. He and Ava worked at a research lab on the harbor, but spent a good deal of time in Cambridge with colleagues.

Rich grinned. "And doesn't he know it."

"Might be a twit, but he's a rich twit," Richard said. "And he knows his wines."

"That's why his interest is amazing at this point, when he hasn't even tasted them," Weezie, the youngest Morgan daughter, said, waving her half-eaten veggie kabob for emphasis.

"But he knows Zeke, and he'd done his research on the old vineyard," Wolfie said.

"Plus he has nothing to lose," Rich said. "If the wine sucks, he walks."

Amy Brennan, Lucy's daughter, listened to the conversation, mouth agape. At sixteen, she was considerably younger than most of her mom's new family members, and she had a huge crush on the twenty-three-year-old Wolfie. Her mother had married Richard two years earlier, and Amy was still adjusting to life as a step-Morgan. She spent part of every week with her dad and his insufferable girlfriend, Chloe Birdsong, who now lived in her father's family home. The only way she tolerated such close proximity to Chloe was being able to go into her old room and close the door. Although she'd lived in the house her entire life, it no longer felt like home, but she did love the view from her window of birdhouses hanging from the huge sycamore tree. "My dad took us to Manning's in March," she said, "when we went up to visit Rob. It was really fancy." Her brother had just completed his first year at Boston College.

Dan nodded. "Yep, it's pretty slick."

Conversation continued on various topics, including the status of the most recent farm acquisitions, two thoroughbreds, four rescued mustangs, and four Hampshire pigs. The latter had been acquired for their meat, but since Weezie had already named them and spent hours regaling everyone about their adorable prick ears, their intelligence, and their exceptional parenting skills, no one expected to see Morgan's Fire bacon or pork tenderloin on the menu any time in the future.

Richard had followed his brother Ben's lead and was now raising thoroughbred horses. Morgan's Fire had also established one the most successful large-scale mustang rescue programs on the East Coast thanks to trainer and farm manager Gus Casey, lured to the East Coast from Arizona. Morgan's Fire mustangs spent a year or so with them and were then adopted either by individuals or riding organizations. Their biggest clients were stables that ran pony camps and programs for children. Once Gus and his crew completed the training, Morgan's Fire horses and ponies were prized for their steady, gentle dispositions.

As Weezie finished yet another story about her pigs, Rich cleared his throat. "Hey, everyone. I have a small something to share. No big deal, but I have to have some surgery next week."

His father jerked his head round, staring at his eldest. "What kind of surgery?"

"Seems I have cancer. Testicular cancer. They say the prognosis is good if you catch it early, which I...they have."

"Who's they?" Richard said. "Not one of the local doctors?"

"Lou Carina. He's a urologist. The surgery will be at the Surgery Center. No biggie. I'll probably go home that day."

"This is very sudden, son. What about getting a second opinion? I know docs at Sloan Kettering, Dana Farber. Some of the top people."

"I know, Dad, but I trust Lou, and the operation is pretty straightforward and simple."

"In my experience, nothing is simple."

"Dad, this is not like Mom."

The others at the table sat silent, watching the two men. They rarely saw the fierce tenacity that had made their father a very wealthy man, but it was always there lurking beneath the surface even in retirement. Now it crackled on the surface, as if sheer force of will could marshal the resources needed to keep his eldest healthy. It hadn't worked for Laura Morgan, and their father had never gotten over what he regarded as his failure.

Lucy stood. "How 'bout some dessert, everyone?" As she began clearing, Ava hopped up to join her.

"Not for me, thanks," Rich said, brushing strands of hair from his forehead. He rose, holding his half-eaten dinner. "I've gotta get going."

Ava set down her pile of dishes and came to hug him. "Please let us know what we can do. Driving? Meals? Anything."

"Thanks," Rich said.

Weezie followed her sister, embracing him. "Bummer, big brother."

"You've got that right," he said, hugging her.

His father came around his daughters and joined in a group hug. "We're with you, son. One hundred percent."

"Thanks, Dad."

"But remember, second and third opinions are a phone call away."

Rich placed his hands on his father's shoulders, startled to see tears rimming his dark brown eyes. "It's gonna be fine, Dad. I promise."

"Course it is." Richard placed a hand on his son's strong jaw. "Love you, buddy. You promise you're gonna keep us posted? I'll call in the morning."

"Promise. Anyway, I'll see you in the morning. Dining room? Ten a.m.? Weekly farm meeting?"

Richard smiled. "Absolutely."

He followed Rich out and stood on the porch as his son walked to his BMW. As Rich's car turned out of sight, Lucy joined him, putting her arm around his waist. "He's going to be fine," she said softly, her head resting on his shoulder.

"Wish I could believe that. Sometimes it seems as though our family's cursed. Just when things are going so well...something like this happens."

"Come on," she said. "Come back to the table. Callie's made floating island, and your grandbabies have joined us."

Richard kissed the top of her head. "*Our* grandbabies."

CHAPTER 5

"Have you given any more thought to returning to college?" Faith Miller asked, giving her youngest what the family called her eagle eye.

"No, for the millionth time," Karen said, taking a bite of the turkey sandwich her mother had just handed her. "This is great, though. Thanks." She waved the sandwich in the air before setting it down and taking a sip of iced tea.

Rex Miller smiled at his daughter. "She's doin' pretty well for herself, Mama. 'Sides, what would we do without her?"

Faith rolled her eyes. "You're a big help. Brick would do just fine on his own. He has to manage half the time anyway with all her part-time jobs."

"Which actually *pay* me," Karen said, shaking the last few potato chips onto her plate and crumpling the bag.

Her mother shook her head as she grabbed the bag and put it in the trash. "Hmm...let's see. There's room and board and the farm credit card that pays for your gas and most of your other needs and recreational activities."

"Well-deserved compensation too," Rex said, patting Karen's hand.

"Thanks, Dad. At least one person around here appreciates me,"

Karen said, blue eyes blazing, face red with indignation. "How much would you have to pay Avery Coggshall or one of his crew to repair all the farm machinery? Not to mention a full-time stable manager or at least co-manager? There are days when my brother *never* appears."

"That's different," Faith said. "Brick's got a family and responsibilities. He needs that job at the hardware store. We're just praying Tack doesn't get pushed out of business by Home Depot."

Rex grinned at his wife. "No one's gonna push Tack Walsh anywhere."

"Tack Walsh is beside the point," Karen said, standing to clear her now-empty plate. "My work for Andy Roby and the paper are my way of earning money. Brick and I worked it out." Aside from her part-time work for the accountant, Karen also wrote an occasional column for the *Crab Gazette* chronicling village events or any number of other topics.

"Hey, sis," Tim Miller said as he banged through the back door with his dark curly hair flecked with sawdust. "Mom, Dad." A woodworker, Tim shared a barn with his best friend, Coop Merrick, the village blacksmith.

"Hey yourself, big brother," Karen said, smiling as she gazed up at him.

"Your face is as red as Dad's tractor. What are you so het up about?"

"Ha-ha... Just enduring the weekly 'when are you going back to college' talk."

"Mom, it's time to let that one go," Tim said, hugging his mother as he grabbed a bottle of water from the fridge.

Faith moved to stand. "Have you had your lunch?"

"Yup. Coop and I ate at the Café. Mobbed, unlike Chez Miller." He waved his hand around the room. "I'm here to borrow a few tools, Dad."

"Well, I'm off," Karen said, brushing by him. "How's Gail?" She referred to Gail Morgan Miller, Tim's wife and one of the eight Morgan siblings.

"Good... Great until she got some bad news about her brother this morning."

"Oh?" Faith said. "Which one?"

"Rich," Tim said. "Apparently, he has testicular cancer. His surgery is next week."

"Poor guy," Rex said.

"So he's told the family," Karen said, more to herself and others.

"You knew?" her brother asked.

Before Karen could reply, her mother said, "I didn't know you two were seeing each other."

"We aren't. I bumped into him in town yesterday."

Tim turned to her. "And he told you about the cancer? He didn't tell Gail till this morning."

"I bumped into him outside the medical building. He looked like he needed a friend. We had lunch, and he told me. No biggie. Spur of the moment. Might've been rehearsal for telling the family. Big families are a bit challenging, you know."

"But also great sources of love and support at times like this," her mother said.

"That's for damn sure," Rex said. "Anything we can do?"

Hands on her hips, Faith nodded. At a lanky six feet, she was all wiry muscle from a lifetime working the farm. Her cornflower-blue eyes flitted from son to daughter as she readjusted the headband holding back salt-and-pepper shoulder-length hair. "Lucy's mom and I can mobilize the Darn Yarner hotline and get meals for him and the family."

The Darn Yarners were a group of eight women, of which Faith Miller and Helen Winthrop, Lucy Morgan's mom, were members. All were in their sixties. For almost four decades, they had nurtured and supported each other and their offspring through difficult times, celebrated many milestones and shared many laughs, tears and adventures. The group still met monthly to swap stories, books, and hobbies. For their children and grandchildren, the Yarners were beloved aunts to whom they knew they could always turn.

Tim raised his hand. "Whoa, Mom. That's super thoughtful, but I don't think we need the Yarner hotline for this. Rich is quiet, and he'll have plenty of support."

"I agree," Karen said, "and I'm late for work. See you all later!"

As she headed for the door, her mother called, "Sweetie?"

Karen turned, expecting more lecturing.

"You are appreciated. By me and everyone here."

"Thanks, Mom," Karen said, smiling as she turned away again. Her father and brother followed, then veered off toward the barn to locate the tools Tim needed.

Karen slid into her truck, a blue-and-white 1962 Chevy pickup that she had lovingly restored. *Poor Rich,* she thought. *So much for keeping things quiet.*

As she pulled into the driveway beside Andy Roby's building, Karen spied Pam Morgan crossing the street. "Hi, there," she called, waving as she hopped out of the truck.

Pam smiled, brushing her strawberry-blonde hair off her cheek. "Hi, Karen. What a day, huh?"

"Beautiful. Have you been gardening?" Karen asked, pointing toward the community garden across the street.

"Picnic lunch in the garden with my fiancé," the other woman said, a blush creeping over her freckled face.

"Sandy Rodriguez is a lucky man," Karen said.

Pam laughed. "I'd have to agree with that."

"How are the wedding plans coming?"

"Slowly, which is fine with me."

As they walked up the steps onto the house's wide-open porch, Pam said, "I was pleased to see you and my big brother spending time together. He needs a friend."

Karen glanced over at Rich's sister. She didn't think it was her place to discuss his health issues without permission. "We just bumped into each other. It was fun to catch up. We all get so caught up in daily life, don't we?"

"I know he told you about his surgery."

"Oh?"

"Sounds like you were really supportive."

"Just tried to listen."

"Well, thank you. It's good for him to reach out to people. He's pretty much a loner."

Karen reached over and squeezed Pam's hand. "He's going to be fine." When she gazed up, she found the other woman's eyes filled with tears.

"It's just tough, you know? After our mother."

"But surely this is different."

Pam nodded. "Yes, of course it is. Well, I see my first afternoon client pulling in, so I better get in and open the office. See you around."

"Yes. See you." She wanted to say more, but she barely knew Rich's sister. In truth, she was a bit in awe of the whole Morgan family. With a nod, she headed to Andy Roby's office as Pam took the stairs two at a time to the second floor.

CHAPTER 6

After a long meeting with his father, Weezie, Gail, Gus Casey, and Wolfie, Rich retreated to the farm office on the second floor of the new barn and closed the door. He loved his family, but felt smothered at the moment. His office space had been completed over the winter, and he was grateful to move into it and out of the temporary office in the farmhouse. *Time to get back to the sanity of work, something I can control,* he mused, digging into a mass of paperwork and making lists for the next few days. As he munched on a tuna salad sandwich Callie had dropped off, his cell phone rang. "Hi, Rich Morgan?"

"Speaking."

"This is Betsy at Doctor Carina's office. Your pre-op is scheduled for ten a.m. tomorrow. Does this work for you?"

"I'll make sure that it does."

"You know how to get to the Surgery Center, right?"

"Yes, thanks, Betsy."

"Any questions for me?"

"Not that I can think of."

"Okay, well, that's set. Be sure to bring your insurance card and photo ID."

"Thanks," he said, hanging up. He ran his fingers through his hair, then tossed the remains of his sandwich into the waste basket. "Here we go," he said aloud to the empty room.

After a few hours' work, he gathered his things. Before standing, he grabbed his cell phone and punched in Karen's number. It went to voicemail, and he left a message asking if she was free for dinner the following evening. He ended with, "Let me know if you're free and have a preference as to where and when we eat. Since it's Friday, I'll make a reservation. Night."

As he headed out, Callie caught him in the front hall. "Hang on a sec," she said, disappearing into the kitchen. When she returned, she held a bag. "Just a few things for supper. Put 'em in the fridge if you don't want them tonight."

"Thanks, Cal," he said, smiling at his father's blonde housekeeper, her Nordic features conveying strength and steadiness. Callie never seemed to age. She'd been with the family for as long as he could remember, and he'd always valued her stalwart presence, especially when their mother passed. At the time, Callie had just lost her own husband, but she was there for all of them through those dark days. Not only did she cook and keep house, but she took over complete care of baby Wolfie after the nanny announced that she couldn't manage a baby and seven others. "See you tomorrow."

"Not if I see you first," she said, hand on his shoulder. "Have a good night."

"You too."

RICH PARKED THE BMW IN THE DRIVE, STARING OUT AT THE RIVER IN front of him. He loved coming home to the quiet and seclusion of the cottage he rented on the peninsula just south of town. Lost in thought and focused on the view, he didn't notice the car parked on the road nearby by nor the woman with dark curly hair seated on his front steps, a basket beside her. As he rounded the car, he looked ahead. "Sara?"

"Hi, you," Sara Gregson called, waving and rising to greet him.

"What are you doing here?"

"Is that any way to greet a friend?"

"But we..."

"Broke up. I know, but I miss you. It's my night off, and I thought I'd stop by, see how you were."

Rich stared at her, unsure of how to respond. On the one hand, he and the petite, lithe yoga teacher were well-suited, both calm, steady, and measured in movement and speech. On the other hand, she irritated and bored him even if he couldn't say why. "Sara... I... I don't mean to be rude, but I'm tired and not the best company right now."

"It's soup, salad, and some delicious bread from the Moon and Stars." She held up the long bag from the town bakery. "No strings, just a meal together. Old friends?"

He smiled. "Sure, okay. Come in."

BEER IN HAND, RICH SAT AT THE COUNTER OF THE TINY KITCHEN, watching Sara, who had tucked a large dish towel around her waist as an apron. As she heated the soup, tossed the salad, and sliced the bread, he mused at how comfortable she was in his kitchen. As she grabbed bowls, plates, and flatware, she turned and noticed him staring. "You're so lucky. This is such a cool house."

"Yeah, it's nice. Can I pour you some wine or something else?"

Hand on hip, Sara gave him a warm smile. "Red would be great if you have it. If not, beer's fine."

They ate at a small round table set in the living room's bay window looking out on the river. The wind had picked up, and white caps dotted the deep blue water. The maritime signal flags hanging from the porch roof slapped against the gutters, curling and uncurling in a colorful dance.

They ate without conversation for five minutes until she broke the silence. "So how are you holding up?"

"You heard."

She nodded.

"Who told you?"

Sara hesitated, soup spoon poised over her bowl, her brown eyes studying his expression. "Your sister."

"Which one?"

"Weezie. It wasn't gossipy. I don't think she knew we'd broken up, or she thought I'd want to know as your friend."

Rich shrugged. "It's okay. I'm sure the whole town knows. I might as well have placed a front page ad in the *Gazette*."

"Now, now... Don't get excited. Back to my original question, how are you doing?"

"Okay. It was a bit of a shock and not what I'd wish on anyone, but they tell me they caught it early and it's very treatable."

"Well, that's good news," she said, extending her hand to touch his. "I'm here for you. I hope you know that."

"That's kind, thanks. As you can imagine, Team Morgan has gone into full operational mode, so I'm pretty well covered."

Sara smiled. "Of course you are, but it's not the same as a loving partner. I want to be by your side through this Rich. I'm serious."

Rich swallowed, setting down a half-eaten slice of crusty bread. "Sara, this is really kind of you, but we did part ways for a reason. I'm not sure this is the best idea right now."

"I disagree, but let's change the subject. How are things at the farm and Morgan Enterprises in general?"

"Never better," he said.

They spent the remainder of the meal catching up on each other's lives. Then Sara insisted on cleaning up. When all the dishes were stacked away and the leftover soup stored in the fridge, Rich said, "It's been great seeing you, but I'm kind of tired, and I've got a few hours of work to do."

"I understand completely. I'll check in tomorrow. Do you need someone to come to the pre-op?"

"All covered, thanks."

"Well, let's touch base this weekend and plan out next week and—"

"Sara, this has been great, but ill or not, I'm not comfortable picking up as if nothing had happened between us. Maybe when I'm on the other side of this, we can have lunch."

She made a pouty face and shrugged. "I love you, Rich. I want you back. I made a mistake, and I want to change it." He started to speak, but she put up her hands in protest. "Don't say anything now. Just think about it, will you?"

With a nod he opened the door. "Night. Thanks again for dinner."

Before he knew what was happening, she stood on tiptoes and kissed him on the mouth, an urgent more-than-friends kiss. Gently, he took hold of her shoulders and stepped back. "Night Sara. Take care."

As she headed down the front steps, she waved over her shoulders. 'I'll give you a ring tomorrow!"

Great. Just what I need, he thought as he closed the door.

CHAPTER 7

At seven Thursday morning, the two friends met at the Land's End stables to go riding. "Hi, stranger," Harriet called, hopping out of her Subaru and waving to Karen, who stood in the yard, two horses saddled and ready to go. "You should have waited for me to help with that."

"We farm folks are up early. Come on. Rebel and Brandi are chomping at the bit." Brandi, a spirited chocolate Arabian, was Karen's horse, and Rebel, a chestnut Morgan, was one of the stable horses used for riding lessons.

Harriet took Rebel's reins and mounted in one fluid motion. "Honestly, it's been heaven to sleep in, even if my husband is up at the crack of dawn." Harriet taught at Hampton Meeting, twenty minutes from Horseshoe Crab Cove, and the school was now two weeks into summer break.

Karen hopped up on Brandi and settled herself in the saddle. "He's the only vet for miles around. His workload should ease if Uncle Deep Pockets manages to lure a resident vet to Morgan's Fire."

"Believe me, Richard's determined. I expect he'll have someone on board before the summer's out. Kyle gave him lots of leads."

"So how are things over at Morganarama?"

"Your guess is as good as mine. I talk to Lucy every day, but she tries to stay out of Richard's businesses including the farm. Merlin's Closet is super busy with summer book fairs and they still haven't managed to replace Wolfie. They really need an assistant. Lynn Casey is filling in a few days a week, and I told them I'd help."

Karen gazed off into space. "Hmm... Maybe I should take on yet another part-time job?"

"Won't things get busy here now that the kids are out of school?"

"More lessons, yes, but it's not too bad."

As they headed onto the Loop Trail, an eighteen-mile riding path that circled the town and peninsula, Harriet turned to her friend. "Are you worried that Morgan's Fire will encroach on Land's End riding programs and all?"

"Not really. Land's End's a working farm. The stables are kind of a hobby my parents support to give my brother and me something to do. Truth be told, he insists on doing everything, which is why I have a bunch of other jobs. I hear Weezie's pony camps are full."

"Yup."

"We stopped those last year. Brick thought they were a hassle, and I got too busy with my 4-H groups to help."

"Those are still going, right?"

Karen nodded. "Sure are. Purely volunteer, but the kids love it. We've got half a dozen raising rabbits, and about the same with goats."

"Kyle told me Weezie's keen on 4-H 'cause they did it as kids in Maine."

"Good luck to her. Kids today have so many other interests."

Harriet nodded. "That's for sure. You guys still give some riding lessons, right?"

"A few to local kids and adults. Aside from our boarders, our riding revenue comes almost exclusively from Mavis's high-end clients, who pay through the nose to ride for a few hours before they head for the spa."

Harriet nodded. "Kyle told me Richard agreed to a 'hands off' with Mavis's clientele."

"Yup, but you know, we'd be fine either way. Our boarders are loyal and have been with us for years. They pay well to have their horses pampered and well fed. There's been a need for another stable in this area for a few years now. We're always turning people away for lack of stall space. Nowadays, the farm's revenue is mostly all the designer produce Mom and Dad grow. The four-season greenhouses they put in two years ago have tripled that yield."

Harriet reined Rebel to a halt. "So how are *you*? Did you have a good lunch with Rich?"

"Can't anyone have any secrets in this town?"

Her friend grinned, urging Rebel forward and over a small rise. "Not many. So?"

"So, it was fine. I'm sure you've heard he's got to have surgery?"

"I did," Harriet said, reining Rebel to a stop as they crested the hill. "How's he doing?"

"Calm, cool, and probably really anxious underneath. He's hard to read. We had a nice time talking in the garden. We agreed to have dinner. He left a voicemail about dinner, but he hasn't called back to confirm."

"He probably has a lot on his mind."

"Maybe. Let's race to Beach Road!" Karen lightly nudged Brandi, and she flew forward. Harriet followed at a slower, more cautious pace. Her friend was a bit of a daredevil, but she was usually careful with the horses, especially on the Loop's sometimes uneven path.

When they were safe on Beach Road, Karen slowed to a trot, and Harriet caught up, frowning at her companion. "You're lucky you didn't fly off and go over the cliff!"

"Brandi can handle anything," Karen said, guiding the horse to the dirt path that ran alongside the paved road.

"You know you could call him," Harriet said. "You don't have to wait around."

"Would you do that?" Karen called over her shoulder.

"Maybe, if I wanted to be supportive and knew he had a lot on his mind."

"I'll think about it. Here comes his sister's fiancé," Karen said as a lone runner approached, veering off the path and onto the road.

Gorgeous in running shorts and a T-shirt, Sandy Rodriguez neared them, slowing down, shielding his dark eyes as he gazed up at them. "Hey, ladies, lookin' good. You're out early."

"You too," Karen said, reining Brandi in.

He wiped sweat from his brow, running fingers through his long dark hair. "Gonna be a scorcher. Should have gotten out an hour ago."

"How are the wedding plans going?" Harriet asked. 'Haven't heard a thing about them."

He grinned. "That's Pam's department. I couldn't care less, as long as she'll be there to marry me on the day."

"My guess is Kyle's uncle has a hand in it too."

"Oh yeah. Richard's all over it. My parents too. Time will tell who survives."

"Well, we'd better get going," Karen said. "I've got a lesson this morning."

"Enjoy your ride," Sandy said, waiting until they moved away to resume his run.

"Isn't Sandy Rodriguez the most gorgeous thing you've ever seen?" Karen whispered as they skirted the town center and rejoined the Loop just west of Morgan's Fire. "Pam Morgan's a lucky woman."

Harriet chuckled. "He's pretty lucky too, if you ask me."

Later, after cooling down the horses, Harriet grabbed her things and waved at Brick Miller, Karen's brother, who was mucking out a stall.

Karen followed her out. "Have a good day."

"You too. Thanks for the ride."

"Any time."

"Call him."

"Who?"

"Ha-ha. What have you got to lose?"

"You're right. With everything he's facing, he might welcome a friendly call back."

Harriet hugged her. "See you, dearie."

Karen slapped the Subaru's hood, then waved. "Count on it!"

~

In the waiting room of the Bayport Surgery Center, Rich read through the simple contracts for two new farm employees. College students home for the summer, they would assist Gus and Weezie with stable jobs and the pony camps starting in two weeks. After nagging her father for two years, Weezie had persuaded him to let her start the camps, which would run in two-week intervals. They had put the word out to local schools, and every camp session was full with waiting lists. Rich smiled, thinking of his sister, full of energy and ideas. *Hope she hasn't taken on more than she can chew,* he mused as his cell phone rang.

"Hey, Rich, it's me, Karen."

"Hi," he said, eye on the reception desk in case they called him. "I'm glad you called."

"I got your message about dinner," she answered brightly.

He smiled. "Great. Listen, just a warning. I'm in a waiting room for the pre-op stuff, so they may call me any minute, and I'll have to go in a hurry."

"No worries. This can be quick. How about tomorrow night?"

"Great, love to. What time?"

"Seven thirty?"

"Perfect. What do you feel like?"

"Do you like the Bluewater?"

"Love it. Shall I pick you up?"

"That'd be great. So you doing okay?"

"Hanging in, thanks. Uh-oh—the nurse just called my name. Gotta go. See you tomorrow night, okay?"

"Of course! Bye."

CHAPTER 8

Lucy and Harriet arrived at the Café at noon, waving to Milly Rodriguez, who was behind the counter. Milly put up one finger in a gesture indicating that she'd be right with them. The sisters made their way to the small side dining room they had reserved.

"There should be seven of us," Lucy said as Josie, the Café owner, set menus around the table.

"Including my best waitress," Josie said. "I'll have Milly bring pitchers of iced tea and water."

"Thanks, Josie," Harriet said.

Soon, all seven of the women were assembled. Milly wrote down their order and disappeared, returning shortly. "Auntie will wave when the food is ready."

Lucy winced. "We'll talk fast. She's not happy having you with us during the lunch rush. Next time, we'll meet in the evening."

Milly waved a dismissive hand. "She's fine. She's just sorry she never joined the Yarners so she could be in on this."

Lucy gazed around the table. Besides Milly and Harriet, Lolly and her sister Marla and Karen Miller waited for her to begin. "So ladies, the first meeting of the Darn Yarners fortieth anniversary has now assembled. I'm hoping our other siblings will join in soon—male and female—but it's time to get started on this. We want our moms to have an amazing celebration and July twenty-eighth is less than six weeks away."

"I just ran into Frankie in town," Karen said, "and she said to remind everyone that they want low-key."

"Our mom said the same," Harriet said.

Lolly guffawed. "Figures, only Mavis would want an extravaganza," she said, referring to her mother, who ran The Cove, an exclusive spa and event venue on the water, east of town.

"Well, I vote for low-key," Karen said. "I know that's what my mom and her sisters would say."

"Richard would love to offer the farm," Lucy said, "either in the barn, or he's happy to erect a circus tent. Apparently, he knows just where to find one."

"I'm sure he does," Lolly said. "That would certainly be in keeping with the low-key theme."

Lucy laughed. "What do you think about hay bales and barbecue?"

Karen clapped her hands. "Perfect, my favorite."

They spent the lunch discussing details of the celebration for the eight women who made up the Darn Yarners. When the group broke up, each had a list of tasks, some of which they planned to foist on their absent brothers and sisters. As the others disappeared, Karen and Harriet lingered outside the Café.

"How are things?" Harriet asked.

"You mean with Rich?"

Her friend nodded.

Karen grinned. "I did it. I called him, and we're having dinner tonight."

Harriet clapped her hands. "Hooray! Good for you. I'm sure he was very pleased to hear from you."

"Don't know about that, but we have a date."

"Where are you going?"

"Bluewater."

"Love it."

"Me too."

"Maybe if this works out, we'll have a double date soon? Kyle loves all his cousins, and he spends a lot of time with Rich."

"Did I hear that the farm's resident vet arrived?" Karen asked as they strolled toward their cars parked alongside Village Hardware at the end of Main Street.

"She has. Kyle is out showing her around as we speak."

"She?"

"Yup. Her name's Kiki Bloom. Kyle and she were in vet school together."

"Have you met her?"

"Nope. Tonight. Lucy and Richard are having a small dinner for her."

"Where's she gonna live?"

"Dad offered her the apartment in the main barn, but it's unfurnished at the moment. I think she wasn't sure if she might not like to live in town. I believe she's staying with family in Bayport for the time being."

They had reached their cars, and Karen threw her shoulder bag into the cab of her truck. "Well, I look forward to meeting her."

Harriet smiled. "I'm sure you'll see her soon, one way or the other. She's agreed to be on call to help Kyle as needed."

The friends hugged, and each hopped into her vehicle. On her way home, Karen mused about the evening ahead and what she'd wear. *Something casual and sexy that won't show all the grease I'll no doubt splatter during dinner,* she thought, heading back to Land's End.

CHAPTER 9

Hands on hips, Lucy eyed her handsome husband, who sat at the kitchen counter conferring with Callie. "A small, intimate welcome dinner, huh?"

"I wanted Kiki to meet the family. Too bad Rob Junior can't come."

"He'll meet her soon, I'm sure. Dr. Bloom is hard to miss."

"She is kinda cute, isn't she?"

Lucy exchanged looks with Callie. "Cute? She's dazzling, even in blue jeans. Every man for fifty miles is going to be after your resident veterinarian."

"Doesn't hold a candle to you two ladies," Richard said. "What do you think, Cal? Are we set?"

"We are," the housekeeper said as she hopped down from her stool. "And I better get to town so I can get back and get cooking. Hope she likes salmon."

"She does. I checked," he said, turning to Lucy. "What's your morning like, my beautiful, dazzling wife?"

"Work. We've got two book fairs this weekend and the mystery weekend coming up in the fall. This summer has gotten super busy!"

"That mystery thing is going to be a lot of work for you, sweetheart."

"You're probably right, but it'll be fun. And, if it's not, this year will be our first and only!"

Lucy and her partner, Lolly, ran Merlin's Closet, a mostly mail-order children's books company. They also ran a number of local book fairs and had a small but growing side specialty selling mysteries for adults. The mystery end of the business has taken off over its first year. So now they were hosting a Mystery Weekend for their avid readers. It was to be held at The Cove, Lolly's mother's estate. They had expected no more than twenty participants, but to their surprise, the count was now at forty-eight. Between the main house and her cottages, Mavis could accommodate thirty. The rest were local or had been parceled out to local inns and B and Bs. They had finally capped the event at fifty.

"I wish you'd let me help you," Richard said, watching his wife move about, gathering her things.

Lucy bent, arms circling his shoulders as she kissed his cheek. "You've got enough to do, my darling, but you're a dear to offer. See you later. I'll try to be home by four."

"How 'bout lunch? I could bring it to you."

"Thanks, but I'm meeting with a bookseller in Bayport."

"You know I could buy Merlin's Closet for an obscene amount of money, and then you'd be a woman of leisure."

"Don't even think about it! Bye!" With that, she banged out the back door, leaving him shaking his head.

"Hey, Dad," Rich said, coming in from the front of the house. "Was that Lucy I heard heading out?"

"Yup. My working wife."

"Shoot. I had a question for her. Do you know the date of this Yarners party?"

"Why do you ask?"

"We've had a request from the Town Council to use the barn for their chicken barbecue and square dance. Apparently, the Legion Hall where it's usually held is being renovated this summer."

"Why don't they just postpone the thing until the hall's put back together?"

Rich eyed him. His father was the most generous, civic-minded person he knew. Ordinarily, he would respond to a request like this with open arms. "What's put a bee in your bonnet?"

Richard grinned. "Ignore me, son. I guess I'm feeling kind of useless these days."

"What are you talking about? You're into everything."

"At the periphery. Like a meddling old auntie. You and Gail handle the businesses, Weezie and Gus manage the farm, Wolfie's running the winery as if he'd been doing it his whole life, and my wife's little book company is suddenly growing by leaps and bounds."

Rich sat beside him at the counter and placed a hand on his shoulder. "These are all good things, Dad. Means you've gotten the best people and set things up to run like well-oiled machines."

Richard shrugged. "Maybe, but this cog feels stuck in a rut."

"Well, that's about to change. That's what I want to talk to you about. I need you. Doctors tell me I'm not supposed to work for a few weeks after surgery. I wanted to go through some things coming up so you can handle them if I'm down for the count."

His father's eyes lit up, and he clapped his hands, grinning from ear to ear. "Well, why didn't you say so? Let's get started."

Rich smiled as he stood up. "Let's get coffee and head over to my office. Sound good?"

After several hours with Rich, Richard excused himself and headed down to the stables. He found Kyle in the stable yard, leaning against a fence and watching three of the wild horses that had arrived the week earlier. The new vet, Kiki, stood beside him.

"A motley crew, aren't they?" Richard said, approaching the two veterinarians.

"Hey, mornin', Uncle Dick."

"Morning. Can't get any luckier than havin' you both takin' care of our newest arrivals. Kiki, how you settling in?"

"Great. My parents are thrilled to have me back home." Dressed in jeans and a cotton shirt, the petite resident vet's ash-blonde hair fell down her back in one long braid, her green eyes sparkling in the sunlight.

"So your living arrangement's working out?"

She smiled. "Temporarily. I'll start looking for my own place once I've gotten my bearings here."

"You know you only have to ask and we'll help with that. The apartment above the barn is yours if you want it."

"Thanks, Richard."

"Of course. So what d'ya think of those three?"

Kyle grinned. "Clearly, the little guy escaped from a circus."

Kiki nodded. "He's a fine little Shetland pony."

"Who bites. Gotta watch him," Gus Casey said, joining them.

"The light brown one looks like an American Azteca. She's a beauty," Kiki said. "And the tall Appaloosa is very cool."

"You know your horses," Gus said. "Not sure what mix is in 'em, but they're some of the more unusual ones they've sent us."

"Have you named them?" she asked.

"Right after they arrived. First thing we do," Richard said. "Little one is Scottie. The black-and-white Appaloosa is Merlin, after my wife's book company, and the buckskin is Rosa."

"In deference to her Mexican roots," Gus said. "We did peg her as an Azteca too."

"Well, group, I've gotta run. See everyone tonight at dinner," Richard said as he turned and headed back to the house. "So glad you're here, Kiki!"

CHAPTER 10

"Well, don't you look pretty tonight, sweetie," Rex Miller said as Karen appeared on the porch where her parents sat, enjoying the early evening. Faith held a glass of red wine, her husband a beer.

"Just my usual jeans, Dad."

"Hmm," he mother said. "But not quite your attire for a day in the barn, honey."

Karen had dressed carefully in her nicest skinny jeans and a flowing sky-blue muslin top that highlighted her eyes and revealed a hint of cleavage. She wore strappy sandals and silver earrings, a half dozen silver bangles jingling on her wrist. "Well, I'm not going to the barn, am I?"

"Where are you off to?" Rex asked as he spied a car turning into the drive.

"To dinner with Rich. Just casual. We're eating at Bluewater."

"Better ask for a bib so you don't spoil that pretty blouse," Faith said. "New, isn't it?"

Karen turned away, waving to Rich. "See you, guys. Won't be late!" She skipped down the porch steps and met the BMW before Rich had time to park.

"Hey," he said as she scooted in beside him. "You look nice."

"Thanks. You too."

And he did in a crisp linen shirt and khakis. Karen wondered idly if Rich even owned a pair of jeans.

"I was going to hop out and say hello to your parents," he said, waving to the Millers.

"No worries. They're fine," she said.

He gazed over at her, hazel eyes warm. "Okay. Off we go, then."

"I will never in a million years get used to the Morgan version of an intimate dinner on either side of the country," Lynn said as she and Gus stood talking with Kyle and Harriet.

Kyle nodded. "Yup, my folks go all out, Uncle Dick too. Must be in the genes."

"That table is pretty impressive, isn't it?" Tim Miller said as he, Gail, and Coop Merrick joined them in the farmhouse's cavernous family room with its multiple sitting areas and cozy alcoves. "Wonder who built it for him?"

"A woodworker in Maine," Gail said. "It seats thirty if needed."

"We're almost that with the kids," Gus said.

"But they've wisely set up a kid's table in the side kitchen," Pam said as she passed a platter of appetizers. Gus and Lynn's three were playing with Amy, Lucy's daughter, in one of the family room's alcoves that had been furnished with shelving, toys, and kid-sized seating. Also with them were Marta, the nanny and Ava and Dan's three children.

"No Sandy tonight?" Harriet asked Pam.

Pam shook her head, strawberry-blonde strands of hair framing her freckled cheeks. "He's working. They've got a big group, and he needed to be there to introduce them. He may try to stop by later."

"Sorcha's getting so big," Gail said as she watched Amy, who held Lynn and Gus's baby in her lap.

Lynn nodded. "Amy is so good with her too. Ruth's great," she added, referring to their old neighbor, Ruth Penny, a local painter who often sat for the children. "But she doesn't hold a candle to Amy. Wish I could hire her as a full-time nanny."

Kyle reappeared and handed Harriet a white wine. "Hey, Coop," he said, noticing the blacksmith who had greeted their hosts and was now headed their way with a beer.

"Hey, everybody," Coop said, running his free hand through dark red curls. "Not sure I fit in with this crowd."

"Course you do," Kyle said. "Besides, the new resident vet is very eager to meet the village smithy."

Coop grinned, his blue eyes scanning the room. "Hence the invitation, I suspect. Where is the new doc, anyway?"

"That would be her beside Lucy."

Coop's eyes widened. "That's the doc?"

Kyle smiled, winking at Tim. "Sure is. Kiki. She's a looker, isn't she?"

For this remark, Kyle received an elbow from Harriet. "Hush, my Neanderthal husband!"

As they watched, their host took the new veterinarian's hand and was now guiding her in their direction. "Here's our blacksmith. Coop Merrick, I'm happy to introduce the farm's new doc, Kiki Bloom."

"Pleased to meet you," she said, extending her hand, which Coop shook.

"Dr. Bloom, hello. Welcome to town."

"Kiki, please," she said, batting her eyelashes as she continued to hold his hand. "This is kind of a homecoming for me. I grew up in Bayport."

"Surprised we never bumped into you," he said.

"Maybe 'cause we're miles older than Dr. Bloom," Tim said, jabbing his side, a grin on his face.

"I doubt that," she said, finally letting go of Coop's hand. "I was thinking we may want to get you out to the farm next week, if you're free, Coop? I wanted to discuss the shoeing program and a few other things."

"Sure. You name the day and time, and I'll be out."

"Hey, guys, whatcha talking about?" Weezie asked, sidling up beside Coop. She had a huge crush on the blacksmith, even though they'd never dated.

"Horseshoes," Kiki said.

"Oh? That's handled by Gus, Dennis, and me."

Kiki eyed the youngest Morgan daughter and smiled. "Well, it's your lucky day. Now that your dad's hired me to oversee the health of the livestock, I can take shoeing off your to-do list."

Weezie opened her mouth to speak, but her father beat her to it. "It *is* our lucky day. We can iron out all these details when we meet early next week. For now, I think Callie's got dinner all laid out on the sideboards, so let's eat. Come on, Kiki. I'm sure you're hungry."

"Starved," she said as she took her employer's arm.

Lynn turned to Harriet as Kyle whistled. "Glad I won't be at that meeting," he whispered, receiving another elbow from his wife.

"Shush!" she said, giggling.

Lynn smiled at the couple. "I fear poor Gus and Dennis will be doing some refereeing there."

"Oh yeah," Kyle said, following the others into the dining room.

CHAPTER 11

"You really do look lovely," Rich said as he drove down the farm's long drive to the main road.

"Thanks. An improvement over my usual crappy clothes, you mean?"

"No. You always look nice. That blue suits you."

"Well, you look pretty great yourself. How are things?"

"Going okay. Setting the wheels in motion for next week."

"Can I help? Have you got drivers to and from?"

"My father's insisting."

"Of course he is."

The conversation trailed off as they headed onto the coast road. When they arrived at Bluewater Seafood, he parked on the road as the lot was completely full. "Good thing I made a reservation. It looks packed."

"Always is on Friday night," she said, grabbing her small purse and sweater.

"How'd you swing this?" she asked as they settled into one of the nicest tables in the restaurant with beautiful ocean views.

Rich grinned. "Begging was involved and maybe an extra tip."

"Wow, things like this don't happen to me."

"I am my father's son. I may have picked up a few pointers along the way."

"I'm sure. You'll have to tell me someday."

A short, blonde waitress dressed in sneakers, black jeans, and a crisp white Bluewater Seafood T-shirt appeared. "Hey, guys, I'm Penny. Can I get you something to drink?"

They both ordered the Pinot Noir she recommended, and, after rattling off the specials, Penny disappeared.

"What are you thinking?" Karen asked.

"About?"

"Dinner?"

Rich blushed. "Oh, sorry. Mind a million miles away sometimes. The mahi-mahi special sounded good, but I'm sort of in the mood for lobster. How 'bout you?"

She gave him a thumbs-up. "I'm in."

"Want to share an appetizer? The kung pao cauliflower sounds great."

"Love to. Do you like Chinese food?"

"Crazy about it. When we lived in Singapore, our chef was from China. She was an incredible cook. Singapore's a foodie's paradise. So many amazing restaurants. Too bad I was too young to appreciate them."

"Have you ever gone back?"

He shook his head. "Nope, but I'd sure like to someday."

After Penny delivered their wine, she took their orders and scurried off, returning with bibs and their salads five minutes later. "Anything else I can getcha?" she asked.

"No, thanks, we're fine," Rich said.

"Okay. They'll be bringing the cauliflower and some bread soon."

As they sipped their wine and enjoyed the piquant cauliflower, Karen said, "This is nice. I could get used to this."

He smiled. "Me too."

"So is this a date?" she asked, meeting his eyes.

"I guess it is."

"Just guessing? Is that code for hedging your bets?"

"No, sorry. I don't mean to be evasive. I enjoy your company,

Karen. I really do. It's just that—"

She reached over and took his hand. "You have a lot on your plate right now. I get it. When things like your diagnosis and surgery take over your life, there's not a lot of space for anything else until you get beyond them."

"Yes, there is that." Rich paused and met her eyes, eyes that he was drawn to. The woman was already the stuff of his dreams. Even with her reputation as a heartbreaker, he loved Karen's spirit, her warmth, and the abandon with which she seemed to live life. So unlike himself.

"What is it?"

He withdrew his hand from her grasp and squared his shoulders, sitting up straighter. "It's just... Well there's been a development."

"Oh no, did the doctor find something else?"

"No, no, nothing like that. Sara came to see me last night."

"Sara Gregson?"

"Yes. She wants to rekindle our relationship."

"Oh."

When he looked over at her, Karen's body seemed to collapse slightly, as if the breath had been knocked out of her. "I wanted to tell you so there wouldn't be any surprises. Especially not right now."

"Of course. So are you and she back together?"

He shook his head. "No... I don't know. And that's what I told her. I don't know."

"How did you leave things?" Karen took a swallow of wine and then grabbed a slice of warm bread, tearing it aimlessly, then placing it on her butter plate without taking a bite.

"She wants to check in, see how I'm doing, see where things lead."

"Is that what you want?"

He shrugged. "It was very kind of her. I didn't know what to say, so I said okay."

"Okay to check in, or okay to get back together?"

"Okay to keep in touch. She's a friend. In many ways, our personalities are similar. There's an easiness there."

"Unlike a relationship with a hotheaded farm girl."

Rich smiled. "Not at all."

At that moment, Penny appeared with their lobsters. "Here you go, folks," she said, setting down the large platters and bowls for the shells. "Can I get you anything else?"

Karen held up her wineglass. "Another, please."

"What about you, sir? Another wine?"

"No thanks, I'm good," Rich said, smiling up at her.

"Okay, then, I'll leave you to it. Enjoy."

They ate their lobsters mostly in silence. They both declined dessert or coffee. After Rich paid the check, he suggested a walk along the seawall. "It's a nice night for it."

"Thanks, but I feel a major headache coming on. I'd better get home before I start seeing stars, and not the ones up there," she said, pointing upward at the clear evening sky blanketed with stars.

RICH PARKED BY THE FARMHOUSE AND WALKED HER TO THE DOOR. "Thanks for having dinner with me." He bent and kissed her lightly.

She reached out and grasped his arm. "Thanks for taking me. I wish you such good luck with the surgery, recovery, and Sara. I'm sure she'll take good care of you."

"It's not like that," he said.

"Well, when you figure out what it is like, let me know. I'm here if you need a friend. Night, Rich."

Without waiting for him to speak, she stepped inside, leaving him staring at the closed door. Rich sighed. *Well, that went well. Good job, buddy. You've encouraged a woman in whom you're not interested and driven away one who sets your heart, mind, and body on fire.*

Karen ignored her parents, who called from the living room asking about dinner. "All's fine. I'm just tired. Heading for bed," she called.

As she washed up, she gazed in the mirror. Softly, she said aloud, "Figures that the one man who's not swooning at my feet is the one I fall in love with. Serves you right, you hussy."

CHAPTER 12

"All set, son?" Richard asked as Rich opened the door. It was six forty-five Wednesday morning. They needed to be at the Bayport Surgery Center by seven thirty.

"Morning, Dad. It's a fifteen-minute drive. Aren't we jumping the gun just a little?"

"Never know about traffic. Besides, you know I like to get there early."

"Uh-huh, okay. I'm all set. Did you have breakfast? If not, we have time to stop and grab something. I can't eat, but you can."

"Already had one of Callie's spectacular breakfast wraps."

"She spoils you."

Richard smiled, patting his oldest on the back. "That she does. Ready?"

As Richard eased the Range Rover down onto Beach Road, Rich said, "Thanks for taking me. It means a lot."

"You know I wouldn't be anywhere else. I was kind of surprised your girl didn't want to come with us."

"Who?"

"That cute Miller gal."

Rich took a deep breath. "I'm afraid I've messed that up."

"Oh?"

"Sara came to see me last week."

"Yoga Sara?"

"Yup."

"So are you guys an item again?"

"No, but she's been pushing hard to make it happen. I felt I should at least let Karen know. It kind of blew up in my face."

Richard turned to him. "Do you want to be with Sara?"

"No, not really."

"What about Karen? If I'm not being too nosey."

Rich grinned. "You kind of are, but I don't mind. Good to have someone to talk to. I like Karen, I really do, but she has a bit of a reputation for ditching boyfriends. Sara and I have similar personalities. Calm, quiet, maybe a trifle boring, but Karen's a firecracker."

"Is that a bad thing? They say opposites attract."

"Maybe, but since I screwed everything up, the firecracker wants nothing to do with me."

"How do you know that?"

"She made it pretty obvious when we had dinner last week. Now she isn't answering my calls or responding to voice messages. To make things worse, Sara insisted on meeting me for lunch Monday, and Karen walked into the Café while we were finishing up. The minute Sara saw her, she grabbed my arm and leaned against my shoulder. It was quite a scene."

His father whistled. "Sounds like you have your hands full, buddy."

Rich shrugged. "Or empty."

"I suggest you get through this business, rest and recover, then you can figure things out."

"Thanks, Dad." He pointed to the right. "That's the parking for surgery patients.

Patient check-in was almost empty when father and son entered. As Rich headed for the desk, something caught his eye, and he looked to the left. There she was, sun streaming in from the window behind her.

"Karen?"

He approached her, and she stood. "Just wanted to wish you good luck."

Richard stepped back, allowing them some privacy, and informed the receptionist that Richard Morgan was checking in. "We'll just give them a minute, okay?" he whispered.

The receptionist nodded, handing him a clipboard. "When he's ready."

"Thanks for coming," Rich said. "It's so good to see you."

Karen stood and hugged him. "Good to see you too. You ready?"

He gazed down with a soft, warm smile. "Dad's spent all morning bucking me up, so I'd better be."

"Well, I don't want to keep you. Just wanted to say good luck. You're going to do just fine." She took his hands, which were cold. "Make them give you a warm blanket."

"Good tip." He leaned down and kissed her cheek. Then, reluctantly, he let go of her hands and turned away, heading for his father and the clipboard.

"I filled out all the basic details," Richard said. "Just a few things left along with your John Hancock."

The three sat together for several minutes until a nurse appeared and called, "Richard Morgan?"

"Okay, then," Rich said, hugging his father and Karen one more time.

"Good luck, son."

"See you around," Karen said, releasing him.

"I hope so."

"No hoping about it," she said. "You can absolutely count on it. If you need anything, please call or have your dad ring."

After Rich disappeared, Karen turned to his father. "How long do they say he'll be here?"

"Most of the day. Operation's only a few hours, but they'd like to watch him. He had the option to stay overnight, but he wants to go home. I'll take him to the farmhouse and hope we can convince him to stay awhile so we can baby him. Doubt he'll be held down long, though."

"Should I stay, do you think?"

"That's up to you, honey. I know seeing you just now did him a world of good. He's pretty fond of you."

Karen looked up to spy tears in Richard Morgan's dark brown eyes. "He's going to be fine, Mr. Morgan."

He nodded, unable to speak. Finally, he said, "Love him, that's all. Wish I could have the operation for him."

"Let me just step outside and make a few calls. Then I'll come sit with you. Can I get you anything? Coffee? A snack?"

"No, thanks, honey. Callie packed a load of supplies, and I have my book and some paperwork in the car. I'll go fetch them, and I'm happy to share. There's enough food and drink for an army. I think Callie prepared for a weeklong siege."

Karen smiled. "Be back soon."

CHAPTER 13

Shortly after noon, Dr. Carina appeared in rumpled green scrubs, his surgical cap slightly askew. "You must be Rich's father," he said. "I'd recognize those eyebrows anywhere."

"Trait my poor son inherited,' Richard said, rising to shake his hand. "This is a dear family friend, Karen Miller."

Carina nodded, but did not move to shake her hand. Turning back to Richard, he said, "He came through fine. We removed the testicle and took a sampling of the lymph nodes. We'll know more when the lab results come back in a few days. He did lose more blood than we like during the surgery. This is relatively common. Because of this, he'll be in recovery for several hours while we pump him full of fluids and keep an eye on him."

"Of course," Richard said.

"I know he wanted to go home today, but I'd like to keep him overnight."

"Absolutely, if that's best. When can we see him?"

"Let's wait till we get him stable and up to a room. Maybe by four? They'll let you know as soon as possible."

When Carina disappeared, Karen gazed over at Richard. His hands were shaking. She reached over and rubbed his arm. "You heard him. He came through fine."

Rich's tall, handsome father shook his head. "Except for the eyebrows, he takes after his mother. She lost so much blood with every procedure...weakened her...grew sicker and sicker."

"Hey, hey... This isn't like that. Breast cancer's very different. Rich said the doctor said his cancer is very treatable, with very good outcomes."

Richard sank down on a sofa, elbows on knees, and buried his head in his hands. She sat beside him, one arm around his shoulder, the other holding her cell phone. She didn't know Lucy's number, but she texted Harriet, begging her friend to get ahold of her sister and tell her to come to the Surgery Center.

Miraculously, Lucy appeared forty-five minutes later, slipping down on the sofa beside her husband, embracing him. "Hi, there. How you holding up, Dad?"

Richard clung to her. "Not so great, baby doll. You didn't need to come, but I'm so glad to see you. Don't know what I'd have done without this kind, lovely lady by my side."

Lucy mouthed *thank you* to Karen over his shoulder.

His wife's presence cheered him up, and the three pulled out sandwiches from Callie's basket. As they were cleaning up from their midafternoon lunch, Sara Gregson appeared. "Lucy, hi," she said. "Didn't know who I'd find here." She nodded at the others. "Richard, Karen. How is he?"

"Not much to report," Richard said. "We're waiting to visit him in his room."

"Room? I thought he'd be going home?" Sara said. "That's why I'm here. I was going to offer to drive him."

Richard stared at her, his eyes registering confusion. "Well, I... We are."

Lucy stood, crumpling waxed paper from her sandwich. "That's very kind of you, Sara. What Richard means is that we've got that covered. He's coming to our house for a few days to recover, so we'll get him home."

"Oh...okay," she said, smoothing errant strands of her dark curly hair. Dressed in patterned leggings and a flowing white tunic, a large leather satchel over one arm, she looked as if she'd just stepped out of a yoga class. She gazed from one to the other of them. "Would you mind if I stay to say hello?"

Since her husband and Karen seemed to have been rendered speechless by the yoga instructor's appearance, Lucy took over and gestured to a chair. "Why don't we wait and see what they say. He may not be up to any visitors."

Sara looked over at Karen, then shrugged, plopping down. After a few minutes, she said, "Haven't seen you at yoga for a while Karen."

"It's the farm's busy season. I'll get back to it sometime. My Aunt Hope is always nagging." Hope Child, her mother's sister, owned the studio where Sara worked.

The group lapsed into silence for a short while until a nurse appeared. "Mr. Morgan?"

Richard hopped up. "Yes?"

"He's in room 116. Down the hall, follow the blue line to the left. We only have fifteen rooms. You can't miss it. He's still pretty groggy, but he asked to see you. Also a Ms. Miller, if she's still here?"

"Thank you," he said, turning to Lucy.

"You and Karen go."

"What about me?" Sara said.

Lucy turned to her, not quite hiding her irritation. "Why don't you and I wait here? Might be a bit overwhelming to have everyone at once."

Suddenly, Karen found her voice. "Why don't I stay here too? Let Richard check in, let us know how he is."

"I'm off, then," Richard said as he turned and headed down the hall.

The three women waited mostly in awkward silence with a smattering of idle chitchat. Fifteen minutes later, Richard appeared. "He's groggy, but in good spirits," he said, arm around Lucy for support.

"What a relief," Sara said. "Would you all excuse me? I've got to find the ladies' room."

Before her companions could direct her to the bathroom, Sara scurried off. *When you've gotta go, you've gotta go,* Karen mused, watching her disappear down the hallway.

"Not sure what to tell Ms. Gregson," Richard whispered, gazing over at Karen. "But he would like to see you, honey."

"You don't think it will be too tiring for him?"

He squeezed her hand. "I think your presence will be a comfort. You go. Lucy and I will hang here."

"Are you sure?" she asked, meeting Lucy's eyes.

Lucy smiled. "Absolutely. Not sure what to say when Sara returns, but we'll think of something. Go ahead."

RICH OPENED HIS EYES, EXPECTING TO SEE KAREN. INSTEAD, SARA'S face loomed above him. "Hey, sweetie," she said, leaning down to kiss his forehead. "How are you feeling?"

He blinked, wondering if his eyes were playing tricks on him. "Where's my dad?"

"In the lounge. He thought he'd give us some time alone," she whispered.

"What about Karen?"

He felt her arm stiffen as Sara pulled back slightly and sniffed. "I'm not sure. I think she may have taken off."

"That's not what my dad told me."

Sara shrugged. "Maybe she left when he was in with you? Not sure. The most important thing for you to do is rest." She ran her fingers lightly over his brow.

Rich closed his eyes, wondering if Sara had been this irritating when they were dating.

CHAPTER 14

When Karen arrived at the room, she fluffed her hair and pinched her cheeks before popping her head in. Sara Gregson hovered over the bed, stroking Rich's brow, whispering in a soothing voice. "There, there, my love." It appeared that Rich was sleeping, but their intimacy was unmistakable. Karen stepped back into the hallway, back against the cool tiled wall, and took a deep breath. *Definitely not my place*, she thought, turning to go.

She found Lucy and Richard sitting side by side when she returned to the lounge. "That was quick," he said. "Everything all right?"

"He's sleeping, and Sara is with him. I didn't want to intrude," Karen said.

"Did he see you?" Richard asked.

Karen shook her head. "Maybe I'll take a little break? Let them have some private time. I have some calls to make, so I think I'll head out to my truck."

"Don't go," Lucy said. "Richard says he really wants to see you."

Karen smiled at the couple holding hands on the stiff fabric sofa. "It doesn't seem like my place right now, but I'll be around. I'll check back in a little while. No worries." She headed out before they could protest further.

As Karen disappeared out of sight, Richard turned to his wife. "Never pegged Gregson as the hussy type."

Lucy chuckled. "Hussy?"

"You know what I mean. She sneaked off and pushed her way in when he really wanted to see Karen."

"I'm sure Sara cares about him. She's probably been terribly worried."

He shrugged. "Humph."

"Besides, it's not our concern, and we're probably best to reserve judgment and stay out of it."

He gave her a weary smile. "Right as always, my dear."

"I've got to meet Mother and Amy in a little while. Are you going to stay?"

He nodded. "I want to see how things go."

She patted his knee. "Well, don't get too tired. Can we bring you anything? I'm sure the girls or Wolfie would be happy to make a run over if needed."

"Thanks, sweetheart, but I'm fine. I'll call later."

Lucy leaned over and kissed him. "We've got his room all made up for tomorrow, so he'll be nice and comfy when he gets home."

"I love you so much," he said, drawing her closer.

"Love you too," she said as they embraced. "You're the world's best dad."

"They're great kids, all of 'em. I'm lucky."

When Lucy reached the parking lot, she spied Karen's truck. The woman herself was slumped over, head on the steering wheel. When Lucy approached and tapped lightly on the window, Karen jumped.

"Oh sorry, you startled me," she said as she rolled down the window.

"I'm sorry. You okay?"

"Yup. Waiting for a call, that's all."

"I'm sure things will sort themselves out."

Karen smiled. As Harriet's sister, Lucy had witnessed many years of broken engagements and broken hearts at the hands of her sister's best friend. "I doubt it. I haven't exactly got the best track record."

"Maybe because you haven't met the right person until now?"

"And he's with someone else. Someone who appears to be working overtime to get back together."

"Give it time."

"I really like him, you know?"

"I'm pretty sure the feeling's mutual. I've got to go, but I hope you're okay. You staying, or...?"

"After I get this call, I'll head in and check on Richard. I'm happy to spell him if needed."

Lucy tapped the truck door. "Good girl. See you later."

AFTER SPEAKING TO HARRIET AND HER MOTHER, KAREN LEANED BACK and closed her eyes. When she woke, it was just after six o'clock. She grabbed a water bottle, splashed water on her cheeks, and ran a brush through her unruly hair. She was just gathering her things when Sara Gregson came out the Surgery Center door and headed for her car. She walked with a bouncy step, but didn't look toward the truck.

Karen waited until Sara's car exited the lot, then she grabbed her bag and headed inside. She found Richard in Rich's room, sitting quietly as his son slept. He stood and came to the door when he spied her. "How is he?" she asked.

Richard looked tired and drawn. "Sleeping. Barely knows I'm here."

"Why don't you head home. Get some rest. I'll sit with him."

"I've never liked to leave my kids in the hospital alone, even adult ones."

"I'll stay. I can sleep in the chair. I won't leave him. Promise."

"Are you sure?"

Karen nodded. "I want to do it. I'll be fine."

"You are a dear girl. Can I get you anything before I leave? Unfortunately, I sent Callie's basket home with Lucy."

Karen hesitated, then said. "You know, I am hungry. Could you stay just long enough for me to run down to the snack bar and grab something?"

"Of course, honey. Off you go."

When she returned with a turkey wrap, apple, and several bottles of water, there was a large recliner sitting next to Rich's bed. "For milady's comfort," Richard said, waving her into the chair.

"Where did that come from?"

Richard smiled. "I have my ways."

She grinned thinking, *deep pockets.* "Thanks, Richard."

"Can't have you crumpled up in that old chair. They'll be bringing linens and blankets soon."

"Of course they will. Now off you go. I've got my food, bed, and I'm good."

Richard kissed his son's forehead, hugged Karen, and headed out, leaving her to nibble on her sandwich. *Should have stopped at the gift shop for toiletries,* she mused, watching Rich sleep. *Even more handsome in sleep.*

A little later, he woke to the sound of her crumpling her sandwich wrapper. "Hey," he said, reaching out his hand giving her a wan smile.

"Hey, you." She came to sit beside him, taking his hand.

"They said you'd left."

Karen smiled. "Can't get rid of me that easily. You want anything? They should be bringing your supper soon."

"I'm good, thanks. I'm glad you're here."

A few minutes later, a nurse appeared and announced she would be taking his vitals.

"That's my cue," Karen said, standing up.

"You're not leaving," he said, still holding her hand.

"No, but I thought I'd make a quick stop at the gift shop for toiletries."

Slowly, Rich pulled himself up. "So you're staying?"

"Looks like it now that your dad's ordered this incredibly large and comfortable recliner."

"He does that sometimes."

The nurse turned to her. "We have packets of toiletries—toothpaste, toothbrushes, face and body lotion, the whole gamut. I can get them for you or you can check at the nurse's station, end of the hall."

"Thanks," Karen said. She squeezed his hand, before gently slipping hers away. "I'll be back soon."

"Promise?"

"Promise."

CHAPTER 15

"Having you here makes this bearable," Rich said, holding up his arm with the IV, then waving to his hospital dinner.

Karen smiled. "I'm glad."

"I was surprised to see you. I thought you hightailed it this afternoon."

"I kind of did."

"Oh?"

"After your dad came out to tell us you were doing well, I came to the room, but when I peeked in the door, you and Sara were... Well, I didn't want to intrude."

Hazel eyes gazed at her. "I'm sorry."

"Don't be. It was fine. I had some calls to make anyway. So I took a break in the parking lot. When I saw Sara taking off, I figured the coast was clear, so I came back to spell your dad and to see you."

He reached out, hand grazing hers. "Thanks for coming back. I know things are murky for you and me. We've just started something... I'm a mess and—"

She grinned. "Then there's Sara, and let's not forget my reputation."

"Minor obstacles. We'll work through them."

Karen rubbed his arm. "Maybe."

"I wish you could sidle up next to me... Maybe get something started?" He pushed his tray table back. "I'm certainly done with this."

She waved her hand back and forth pointing from him to her. "You may be done with that, but you and I aren't doing this."

He arched one of his bushy eyebrows. "Party pooper."

Chuckling, Karen leaned over grabbing the tray. "Party pooper? That's an expression I haven't heard for a while."

"I'm kind of an anachronism. Leave that tray. They'll come for it, I'm sure."

"No problem. I see a cart in the hall."

When she returned, she smoothed his covers and lay down gently beside him. "Just for a minute. Can I get you anything to drink?"

"Nope. This is what I wanted." He rested his head against her shoulder.

Karen grasped his hand, careful not to disturb the IV. "Me too." She closed her eyes as she felt his regular breathing against her.

"Hi, you two," a voice said, startling her awake. A tall lanky nurse in floral scrubs stood at the side of the bed. Her straight brown hair was tied back in a ponytail, a few strands falling over her face.

"Oh! Sorry," Karen said, hopping off the bed.

"No worries at all. You looked very comfy. Just need to check on Rich. I'm Lisa, by the way. I'll be here all night."

"Hey, Lisa," Rich said. "I was just going to call you for a bathroom break."

"That's what I'm here for," Lisa said, moving closer to him.

"That's my cue to find a ladies' room and wash up," Karen said. "I'll be back soon."

As Rich leaned on Lisa, walking slowly toward the bathroom, Karen grabbed her bag and headed out. By the time she returned, he was back in a freshly made bed, pillows fluffed and wearing a clean johnny. She noticed a pile of linens, pillow and blanket had been placed for her on the recliner.

"That was quick," she said.

He smiled. "Just call me Flash. Feels great to get cleaned up."

While Lisa took his vital signs, Karen made up the recliner. When the nurse left, she gazed over to see his eyes drooping.

"Some exciting company, huh?" he asked, giving her a sleepy grin.

"You're perfect," she said, rubbing his arm. "I just wish you'd go to sleep, 'cause I'm pretty tired."

"Liar. What is it, six thirty?"

"We farmers go to sleep at dusk and rise before dawn."

"I don't believe you, but I'd sure like a good-night kiss."

Karen leaned over and kissed him softly. As his hand stroked her cheek, Rich let out a sigh.

"Good night," she whispered, hands on his chest. "I'll be right here if you need anything."

"Just you. I'm sorry, but there'll probably be a cast of thousands throughout the night." With that, he closed his eyes and slept.

CHAPTER 16

Karen woke shortly after six, still holding Rich's hand. She gazed over to find him awake and watching her and sat up abruptly. "Oh! Was I snoring or talking in my sleep? I do both."

He gave her a sleepy smile. "Peaceful as a lamb, but much prettier. I could watch you all day."

"I very much doubt that." She set her blanket aside and ran fingers through her hair. "I must look a fright."

"Not to me," he said as the door opened and Sara Gregson stepped into the room.

Her eyes roamed from one to the other. "Doesn't this look cozy."

"You're up early," he said.

"Wanted to see you before I teach my early class. I see someone else got here first. Morning, Karen."

Karen eased out of the recliner, taking the sheet and blankets with her and setting them on a chair. She grabbed her bag. "Why don't I give you two some privacy."

"You'll come back?" he said.

"Will do." *Although I'd like to be a million miles away,* she thought as she closed the door behind her.

A new nurse was doing her rounds, and it appeared that she would soon be interrupting the pair in room 116. After washing up,

Karen returned to find Sara and Rich talking over his breakfast tray. The recliner had been shoved into the far corner, and Sara sat on the only other chair in the room. Swallowing hard, she approached the bed. "Anything good?" she said, endeavoring to keep her voice light and cheerful.

Rich looked up and smiled. "Not bad. You hungry? Plenty of toast and a whole bowl of cream of wheat. These eggs are plenty for me."

"Thanks, but I'll grab something when I get home."

"You're not leaving, are you?"

Karen came to the opposite side of the bed and touched his hand. "You two seem to have things covered."

"Sara's leaving soon to teach her class, aren't you?"

"I got Tessa to cover," Sara said, her brown eyes twinkling.

"When?"

"Just texted her."

Rich frowned before turning back to Karen. "Don't go."

She leaned forward, smoothing hair from his forehead, kissing him lightly on the cheek. "We farmers have work to do. Sara will take good care of you. And I imagine within the hour, there'll be a room full of Morgans. Is your dad picking you up?"

He nodded.

Both of them were oblivious to the woman sitting next to him until she spoke.

"Why don't I give him a call? I can certainly stay and bring you home."

Reluctantly, he turned away from Karen. "No worries, we've got this Sara. Thanks anyway."

"Well, I can plump up your pillows and watch out for you till he arrives at least," Sara said, giving Karen a look that screamed *get out!*

Karen chuckled. "That's my cue. Good luck this morning. I'll check in later."

"Promise?" he said.

"Promise," she said, hugging him gently.

As she drove home, Karen couldn't decide what to make of the situation. She was falling for Rich Morgan. *Hard.* But the truth was, she didn't know him well enough to know what he felt about her. Now with Sara Gregson popping up everywhere, the whole relationship felt a little crowded. *This is usually where I cut and run. Whenever things get messy, mushy, or complicated, I'm gone. For some reason this time it's a tough call.*

"Well, here's our Florence Nightingale," Faith Miller said as her daughter banged in through the kitchen door.

"Hey, Punky," Rex said. "Pulled an all-nighter, huh?"

"Morning Mom... Dad."

"That was kind of you to stay with him, honey," Faith said. "You probably need a nap."

Karen sat down and grabbed a piece of toast from the wrought iron toast rack. "Au contraire. Thanks to the deluxe recliner Richard Morgan had brought in, I slept like a log."

"Pays to have bucks," her father said, grinning, his blue eyes full of mischief. "What's your plan today, Punky?"

"After I help Brick with the stables, I've got to go into town. Andy has a bunch of work for me and a million errands. Having lunch with a couple of Darn Yarner-ettes."

"Excuse me?" her mother said, eyeing her.

"I just thought of it on the way home. I'm gonna suggest we start calling ourselves the Yarner-ettes. Catchy, huh?"

Rex clapped his hands. "Very. How's the big do comin' along?"

Karen winked at him. "Can't say with one of the DYs present."

"All right, you two. That's enough of DYs and Yarner-ettes! Now, what happened with your guy? How is he?"

"He's not my guy, he's fine, and he has a girlfriend."

Faith frowned, waving her spoon. "Maybe not? The girlfriend, I mean. After all, who spent the night at the hospital with him?"

"Mother, give it up. A friend stayed the night, then his *girlfriend* appeared and took over."

Faith gazed from husband to daughter. "She sounds kind of pushy."

Karen shrugged. "You probably know her better than I do."

"Hmm... I'll ask Hope about her today."

"No, you won't. Leave it alone! Please, Mom."

Faith huffed, eyeing her husband. "Well, I've got work to do, and so do you. Sweetie, can I make you some eggs before I head out to the barn?"

"No, thanks. This toast and a banana'll do. I'll grab coffee in town. See ya."

She ran upstairs, changed into her work jeans and a T-shirt, and headed out, avoiding the kitchen and any further conversation about her guy.

CHAPTER 17

Rich closed his eyes, leaning back in the bed that had been his since their early days in Maine. Exhausted after a long morning, he had mixed feelings about where he found himself. On the one hand, it was wonderful to have support and Callie's cooking. On the other, he missed the quiet of his rental on Beach Road with the cries of gulls and the soothing sound of waves lapping the shore. His home was his retreat from the bustle of a big family, and he cherished his solitude. *Probably best to be here*, he thought as he drifted off. *If I was home, Sara would have moved in. I'm really going to have to do something about Sara.*

When he woke an hour later, he could hear voices in the front yard. Gingerly, he slipped to the side of the bed. The meds appeared to be working, as he was no longer in much pain. He hobbled to the window and spied Weezie chatting with Coop, Tim, and Karen. His father had mentioned that Coop and Tim would be delivering furniture and lamps today, so he wasn't surprised to see them. Karen, on the other hand, yes. He opened the window wider, and the group turned and looked up as one.

Hands on hips, Weezie frowned. "What are you doing out of bed, brother dear?"

"I'm not dead."

Tim waved. "Looking good. How do you feel?"

"About how you'd expect," Rich replied. "And that's all I'm willing to say on the subject."

Karen gazed up, shielding her eyes from the bright afternoon sun. "You up for a visitor?"

"Give me five minutes and I'll come down."

His bedroom door opened behind him, and his father stepped in. "Oh no, you won't. Dr. Carina said bed rest for at least two or three days. You can entertain your lady friends up here." Richard went to the window and called down, "Give us a few minutes, honey. I'll come fetch you when he's decent."

Rich groaned. "Decent? What am I, sixteen and getting ready for the barn dance?"

"No, you're a thirty-five-year-old mule who doesn't realize that he's recovering from surgery. Come on, let's get you decent," he said, waving toward the bathroom.

"You've got quite a support team, don't you?" Karen said. They sat in the second-floor sunroom on the soft, upholstered cushions of a wicker settee.

"Tell me about it," he said. "They mean well, but I don't do well with hovering. They won't bring me my briefcase either, which is really pissing me off." Karen gave him one of her two-hundred-watt smiles. The ones that turned his insides to mush. *God, she's pretty!*

"You're not supposed to be working. Doctor's orders."

"I wish I could take you to lunch or dinner."

Karen smiled. "This isn't going to last forever."

"Don't tell me you're talking about you and me?"

She shook her head, reaching over to rub his shoulder. "I meant your convalescence, but as for the other, I think it's best that you and I stay friends and nothing more. I can't lie and say I wasn't interested in more, but I think you've got your hands full with recovering and your relationship with Sara. Until you figure that out, I'm going to step back."

He gazed out the wall of windows with their magnificent views of the fields and river. "I never realized you could see the winery barns from here," he said absently, changing the subject.

"It's gorgeous, and what a great idea to have this sunroom up here."

He nodded. "We had one in Maine. Our mother's idea when they renovated the house. It was her favorite room, especially those last months before she died. It was huge, almost ran the length of the house. When they'd let us, the older kids would bring sleeping bags and camp out with her in the sunroom. There were long tables always covered with a jigsaw puzzle or two in progress."

"Sounds magical," Karen said, glancing over, noticing sadness in the depths of his beautiful eyes.

"It was. Surreal too. You're right, of course. I'm a mess right now, and I need to figure things out with Sara."

"Yes, you do. Now stop worrying, rest up, and get better."

They chatted about town gossip and Karen's work. Sometime during the conversation, he had reached over and taken her hand, which he was still holding when his brother Teddy popped his head in. "Hey, bro...Karen. Am I interrupting?"

Karen squeezed Rich's hand before releasing it and standing up. "Not at all. I've gotta get going."

The second Morgan brother was the opposite of Rich, his sandy hair tousled, pale blue eyes the color of the sky. His broad shoulders and powerful build were well suited to his days working with the heavy metal sculptures he created, most for parks and outdoor installations.

"No Gerry?" Rich asked, referring to his brother's partner, who was a successful mural artist. Many of the commercial buildings in Providence had murals by G.W., as he signed his work. Teddy Morgan and Gerry Winters were well known in the city's vibrant arts community and their work was beginning to receive national attention.

"Nope. Someone's got to work. The condo fees go up every month. So how are you?" Teddy asked, stooping to embrace him before flopping down on the sofa, which gave a creak as he landed.

Karen watched the interplay between the brothers, imagining them camped out beside their ailing mother. Big families could drive one crazy, but they were also there for you. She and her siblings were thankful every day to have each other and both their parents still vital and active. "I'll leave you guys to it, then. Take care of yourself," she said, eyes warm as they met Rich's.

"She's a cutie pie, isn't she?" Teddy said shortly after Karen departed.

"Cutie pie?" Rich gave his brother a look with arched eyebrows.

"You guys an item?"

"No, just friends."

"What about the lithe, lovely yoga instructor?"

"Sara. We're in limbo."

"Come again?"

"We broke it off a while ago, and now she suddenly wants to rekindle the romance."

"So what about you?"

Rich shook his head. "Hell if I know. I mean, I like Sara, but I was kind of relieved when we went our separate ways. There was something missing, you know? She's a good soul, but..."

"Sounds like your grandmother."

Rich laughed, then winced with pain. "No jokes. It hurts to laugh. Can't tell if Sara's behavior is a Florence Nightingale thing or genuine."

"What about cutie pie?"

"Friends, I told you," Rich lied, not sure what to say about his feelings for Karen. *Yes, we're friends, but a part of me would like to be a hell of a lot more.* "Can we get off the subject of my boring love life, please?"

As they chatted, the brothers were joined by Ava and Pam, who brought sandwiches. Then Wolfie stopped in for a few minutes.

Noticing Rich's eyes begin to close, he invited the gang to head out for a winery tour. "Let's leave the poor guy in peace."

As his siblings departed, Rich leaned back, closed his eyes, and thought about Karen. It was Karen he dreamed about, not Sara. Karen who put his libido in overdrive, Karen who touched his heart. What did that say about his feelings for Sara? Or was it just that Karen was someone new? *I am really screwed up,* he thought as he drifted off to sleep.

The next thing he heard was Sara's voice, whispering, "Hey, sweetie."

Rich opened his eyes and found her beside him.

CHAPTER 18

After leaving Rich and Teddy, Karen strolled down to the stables to say hi to Weezie and see the new mustangs. Kiki Bloom the new vet was there, ministering to Cracker, one of the stable horses. As Karen drew near, she saw that the vet had wrapped one of the horse's legs with a support bandage. "Oh gee, what happened?" she asked Weezie, who stood nearby.

Tears in her eyes, Weezie said, "Torn tendon. My fault. We worked her too hard with lessons, and then she mixed it up with one of the mustangs."

"Bummer," Karen said, rubbing Cracker's jowl. She loved the gentle American paint breed and was always begging her parents to acquire one for Land's End. "Hey Cracks, how you doin'?"

"She'll be fine," Kiki said, standing and stretching. "Ice and heat will do the trick."

"How are the new mustangs doing?" Karen asked, directing her question to Weezie.

Before Weezie could reply, Kiki said, "Great. Won't be long before we can get our gorgeous smithy out here to shoe 'em."

Weezie rolled her eyes and gave Karen a look.

Karen gazed from one to the other. "I wouldn't think you could do that for many months."

Kiki waved her arms and hands. "Kidding! Just have to think of another excuse to get Mr. Merrick out here."

"I would imagine he's been out a good bit with all the furniture and lamp deliveries," Karen said.

"Not enough," the vet said, cleaning up her instruments and materials. "Well, no rest for the weary. I've got a private client in town with a sick cat. Kyle asked me to take it. See ya."

As Kiki strolled toward her cherry-red Rav 4, Weezie turned to Karen. "Good vet, but a pain in the ass."

Karen leaned against the fence, shielding her eyes from the sun. "She moves fast. Have she and Coop got something going already?"

"Only in her mind. As if Coop would care two hoots about her."

Karen shrugged. "Don't know the woman, but she is pretty."

"If you like pinched-faced Barbie dolls. Come on, I have waters in the office."

Karen chatted with Weezie for a while, then headed up to her truck. As she drove out, she passed Sara Gregson's white Honda. *Got away in the nick of time. Thank God Harriet and I planned a hiking trip for next week. It'll be great to get out of town for a while.*

After a Friday breakfast meeting of the Darn Yarners fortieth anniversary party, Karen headed home to pack. She and Harriet had planned the eight-day hiking trip months earlier. Thanks to a Maine friend, they had snagged a cabin in Acadia National Park, an almost impossible feat for nonresidents. They'd invited Kyle to join them, but he declined, insisting they have a girls' adventure. As she packed, Karen mulled over the situation with Rich and decided she had made the right decision for her. There was something different about him than the other men she had dated and to whom she had been engaged. She felt sure if she allowed things to go further, she could easily wind up with a broken heart. *Better to nip it in the bud,* she thought, zipping up her very full duffel.

"So you're leaving us, Punky?" Rex Miller asked, leaning back in a kitchen chair, watching Karen fill a canvas satchel with provisions.

"And emptying our larder on her way out," Faith said. "Leave us something for dinner, please."

"Ha-ha, I'm only grabbing a couple of things. We'll stop at a grocery store up there." Karen stuffed a bag of apples into the overflowing bag.

"I'm sure Harriet has a stash of provisions just like that, doesn't she?" Her mother eyed her, hands on hips.

"Of course she does. In fact, her wonderful husband packed it for her."

Faith nodded. "That boy is one of a kind, isn't he?"

"Okay, then," Karen said, stopping to hug her father, then embracing her mother. "We'll be home next Friday."

"Friday?" Faith said. "I thought you only had the cabin for five days."

"We do. We're coming south to Freeport for the last few days. Shopping, hiking, and a spa."

Her mother rolled her eyes. "Must be nice."

"Says the woman who's traveled all over the globe the past couple of years."

Faith put up one finger. "Three trips, my sweet girl. Besides, it's yours and your siblings' fault. The trip you gave us woke the travel bug." Two years earlier, the Miller siblings had pulled together and sent their parents on a trip to Europe. Faith and Rex had taken two more trips since then.

"Let the girl go, honey," he said. "Have fun, Punky."

"Thanks, Dad. See you both next week! I'll call and let you know how we're doing, but I understand cell phone service is spotty in Acadia."

Her mother blew her a kiss as Karen headed out the back door to find Harriet waiting beside her green Subaru, rear door open. "Ready?"

Karen waved. "So ready. Can't get out of this town fast enough."

Her friend gave her a questioning look, but stayed silent.

CHAPTER 19

Their last day in Acadia, it rained buckets, forcing them to huddle inside with a fire and lots of reading materials. "Much as I've loved every day of hiking, this is *really* nice," Harriet said, leaning back in a comfortable chair covered in soft plaid flannel.

"No argument from me," Karen replied, picking up her copy of the latest Anne Greyson mystery. "I wish we could stay another week. It's been really fun."

"Well, we still have Freeport and Wolfe's Neck," Harriet said. "And our day of shopping. Even though it's my least favorite thing to do, I'm dying to hit the outlets. I need all kinds of things, including a dress for the wedding. I'd also love to pick up some new quilts. Ours are in shreds."

"You're so lucky," Karen said dreamily. "Kyle's such a great guy."

Harriet eyed her friend. "Yes, he is. You're going to find the right someone, dearie. I know you are."

"Maybe. My track record so far is pretty dismal. It figures the one guy who feels like 'the one' is with someone else. Serves me right."

Harriet put her book down and sat up. "Don't talk like that! Besides, I'm not convinced we've heard the last of Rich Morgan."

Karen rolled her eyes. "Calm down, Pollyanna. That ship has sailed with Ms. Yogi at the helm. They're perfect for each other."

"Pardon the expression, but bullshit. I like Sara, and she's a great yoga teacher, but I don't see Rich and her staying together long-term."

"Oh? Why not?"

"Because I've seen the way he looks at you."

"That was before Sara came back on the scene. Let's not talk about this. It's giving me a headache."

"All I'm saying is—don't give up. I figured I'd be single forever, especially after the nightmare of Louis, but then I met Kyle, and I've never been so happy." She referred to the grifter who had wooed her in college and stolen her inheritance and many of her most valuable possessions. Eventually, Louis and his accomplice had been brought to justice and some of Harriet's possessions recovered. More importantly, his capture had begun her healing process, along with the fierce love of her future husband.

"Trouble is, I really like him," Karen said, gazing over at her friend with tears in her eyes.

"I know you do," Harriet said quietly. "I've never seen you light up when you talk about a man like you do when you're talking about Rich. That includes your two former fiancés."

Karen shrugged. "Pathetic, huh?"

"I haven't given up on Rich, and you shouldn't either."

"Don't have much choice, do I?"

Harriet grinned. "Maybe there'll be some eligible bachelors at the Darn Yarners party?"

"You forget, I live here. I know every single guy from Bayport to Leeside."

Harriet set down her book and hopped up.

"Where are you going?"

"Lunch. Can I make you something?"

Karen chuckled. "How about a big plate of crow?"

THE FARMHOUSE WAS ABUZZ WITH PLANS FOR PAM AND SANDY'S "low-key wedding." As Rich grew stronger, he closeted himself in the second-floor sunroom to avoid the fray. The second week of his stay, he was up and around, so he retreated to his barn office between meals. Sara had been out almost daily to check in and had driven him to town for errands and to pick up clothes and items from his house. On the one hand, he was ready to move home, but Callie's cooking was a godsend, and his family, crazy as they were, provided some buffer from Sara's hovering.

When he moved home, he feared Sara would attempt to move in with him. He enjoyed her company, but also knew the time had come for them to talk about where they were going. He loathed conflict and had just let things slide, but he knew he needed to act. He had heard Karen and Harriet were back from their trip. His chest ached when he thought of Karen, but he knew the only fair thing to do was keep his distance.

After several hours working, he closed up the office and headed out. Instead of walking back to the house, he decided to stroll down to the stables. When he rounded the barn, he spied his sister talking to Gus Casey, who stood beside Tornado, one of the wild horses that had been with them since the beginning. All Tornado's original stablemates had been adopted, but Gus felt the black stallion was still too wild. He had also grown quite attached to the enormous horse. No one else could handle him like Gus.

"Hey, guys," Rich said, waving as he approached.

Hands on hips, Weezie gazed at him. "What's management doing down here with the little people? You okay?"

"Not ready to ride that brute, but coming along. How's the training going?" he asked, turning to Gus.

"He'll take a saddle, but he's a bit picky about who rides him," the trainer said, rubbing Tornado's silky muzzle.

"No one rides him but Gus," she said. "I'm trying to convince him to let me try."

"Not without the boss's okay."

Rich winced, fearing that the next words out of his sister's mouth might be something like *I'm the boss down here,* but she mercifully said nothing. He smiled at his sister. "Dad's right, and he should know." Not long after Tornado's arrival, the horse had reared up and given Richard a nasty kick in the head. "There are plenty of other ponies in the barn."

"Well, I'm going to have to ride him someday, or he'll never be eligible for adoption."

They chatted for a while before Rich said goodbye and turned to go. "Will I see you at dinner, sis?"

Weezie looked up, grinning. "Nope, I have a date."

"Oh?"

"Coop's taking me to dinner."

"Oh, he is, is he?" Rich exchanged looks with Gus, who shrugged. "When did this start?"

"We arranged it this morning before the pushy Dr. Bloom arrived, thank goodness." She turned away, waving over her shoulder as she headed into the barn. "See you, big brother!"

Rich shook his head. "What's that all about?"

Gus grinned as he held up his hands. "Don't ask me. There's been a bit of a tug-of-war over the village smithy. Dennis and I try to stay out of the line of fire."

Rich laughed. "Coop must be like a pig in shit."

Gus led Tornado around the corral, his voice soft. "I don't think he knows what to make of it."

"We never do. See ya."

Rich walked slowly up to the farmhouse. *Time for a nap,* he thought. *Maybe I'll dream of Karen.* As he neared the kitchen door, he spied Sara's Honda coming up the drive. *No rest for the weary,* he sighed, veering off to circle the house and meet her.

CHAPTER 20

The fortieth anniversary party celebrating the eight Darn Yarners was underway. "Who would have thought forty years ago that anyone would be celebrating us old broads," Belle Pollart said, her brown eyes sparkling as she hugged Faith Miller.

Karen stood beside the two women, Belle's son Billy and his girlfriend, Aisha, nearby. Karen and Billy had gone all through school together, he being only one of three students of color in the school unless you counted the Rodriguez clan. Billy and his father, Will, ran the town docks and fishery and Belle the fish market near the main pier. Billy met Aisha in Boston, where they both attended BU. Now Aisha worked alongside his mother at the market and sometimes on the boats. Both women were strong and muscular as well as beautiful. Belle's lovely oval face was unlined, her curvaceous figure evident in a light, floral sundress.

"Where's your handsome hubby?" Faith asked.

Belle laughed. "Headed for the bar, where else? We so seldom get a day off, and he intends to take full advantage. You're looking well, Karrie."

Billy and Karen had been inseparable in grade school, and his mother had given her the nickname. No one else ever called her

Karrie. "Thanks. You too. Can't believe I haven't bumped into you all summer."

"It's been crazy," Billy said. "So many new fishing permits and boats. Just when we thought things would slow down with all the restrictions, people are pulling in monkfish and all kinds of other exotics to ship overseas."

Karen made a face. "Not a fan of monkfish."

Aisha laughed. "It's an acquired taste. Shall we youngins head for the bar? Can we get you something?" she added, turning to the mothers.

"No thanks, sweetie," Faith said. "I think we need to corral the rest of the old bags and find a spot to enjoy this shindig together."

Karen linked arms with Aisha and Billy followed them. As they walked across the grass to the bar just outside the barn, she said, "We really have to make plans to get together. I miss you guys."

"Ditto," Aisha said as they practically ran into Rich and Sara.

"Hey, hi," he said, looking from Karen to her companions.

Before Karen could respond, Sara said, "Hey, girl," to Aisha, giving her an exaggerated thumbs-up.

"Hi," Aisha said, looking a bit taken aback at the effusive greeting.

Sara turned to Rich. "Aisha's one of my best students."

Karen found her voice at last. "I'm not sure if you guys know each other? Rich Morgan, this is Aisha Daniels and Billy Pollart."

Rich extended his hand, first to Aisha, then to Billy. "Hey, I've heard about you from my sister Ava and her husband, Dan. Not much of a boater, but I've bought fish from your mom," he added, looking at Billy.

"Aisha works there too," the other man said.

Rich smiled at Aisha. "I'll be sure to look for you next time I'm in." He turned to Karen. "How have you been?"

"Fine. And you?"

"On the mend. Moving back home next week."

"Great." It felt to Karen as if they were in a bubble, just the two of them, the rest of the party outside, muted and far away.

"I'll miss Callie's cooking, but it's time."

Karen smiled. *Oh, how I've missed you, Rich Morgan*, she mused, longing to throw her arms around his slender frame and hold him tight. "I'm sure she'd deliver 'meals on wheels' every day if you asked her to."

"Oh, I'll be handling that," Sara said, grasping Rich's arm as she rested her head on his shoulder.

An awkward silence followed until Billy said, "Hey, guys. We were about to get a drink. Want to join us?"

Rich looked at Billy, then Karen. "Thanks, but I'm apparently needed in the house. We were just headed that way."

"See ya!" Sara said as she led him away.

Aisha leaned close to Karen and whispered, "What was that about? Who does she think she is?"

Karen shrugged.

"I've taken like three classes from her. Besides I much prefer Sasha's classes."

"Isn't she the one who does hot yoga?"

Aisha nodded. "Love it, love it, love it! After a day at the market, it's just what I need."

"I'm afraid I'd pass out," Karen said.

"Maybe the first few times, but then you get into it. It's amazing."

"Hey, you two yogis," Billy said. "What do you want to drink?"

"WE GOT LUCKY, LADIES," FRANKIE BROWN SAID, GAZING AROUND THE oval table at her fellow Darn Yarners. "What a night."

She shared the table with Lucy's mom, Helen, Mavis LaSalle, the three Childs sisters, Faith, Hope, and Grace, Belle Pollart, and Rosa Rodriguez. "Can't believe it's been forty years," Mavis said. "Where did they go?"

Helen smiled, gazing around at her dear friends, the friends who had brought her through the nightmare of her divorce and helped her build a life for herself and her four young daughters. Frankie in particular had been her bulwark, moving into the cottage for months to help with the kids. "I can't claim forty," she said softly, "but the past twenty-eight years have been the happiest of my life. I wouldn't be here now if it weren't for all of you." Tears in her eyes, she reached over and squeezed Frankie's hand.

"Right back at you, girl," Mavis said. "Excuse my language, but divorce sucks."

"Let's not go there today," Faith said. "My sisters and I have come up with memories for each of the forty years. We wrote them down and wanted to share with you all so the group can add and fill in where we've forgotten stuff."

Hope, Grace, and Faith passed around beautiful journals covered in embossed flowers. When each opened her book, several sheets of floral-trimmed paper fell out with the forty-year list.

"Oh, you three," Rosa said, tearing up. "This is such a special gift!"

"Skinny-dipping at Miller's Cove!" Belle cried, reading her copy. "Oh, wasn't that a fun night?"

"Many fun skinny-dipping nights," Mavis said. "I can't believe we all managed to find babysitters in those days. Fortunately, some of you had husbands."

Frankie laughed. "Surfing lessons! We should definitely do that again."

"Too many martinis at Ballards!" Helen chuckled. "Oh dear, isn't that the truth?"

"Oh my goodness," Rosa said, blushing. "Skinny-dipping off Sebring Park and getting caught in the act by Tack Walsh! I still can't look him in the eye. I usually make an excuse and have Cesar or one of my kids go to the hardware store just so I can avoid him."

"We are so lucky we didn't get smashed against the seawall and killed," Hope said. "No one ever swims there."

Her sister Grace shook her head. "Especially not naked."

Frankie waved her list. "But, if we hadn't had that escapade, we'd have never thought of creating the park." She referred to the lovely green space by the ocean, made possible through the hard work of the Darn Yarners, their seed money, and their many fundraising projects to support its creation and maintenance.

"Very true," Helen said. "Are we planning to share these with the other guests tonight?"

Hope shook her head. "I don't think so. No!"

"Agreed!" her sisters chimed in.

"These are *our* memories... Our gift to you all," Faith said. "It will give us something to do at future meetings, filling in all the things we've forgotten."

CHAPTER 21

Karen, Lucy, Harriet, and Milly Rodriguez were in charge of decorations while Pam and Gail had taken care of catering. Sandy had found the band, a local country western band that their mothers loved. Lolly had secretly worked with Kendall Reese, her mother's chef, to create an enormous sheet cake that depicted the area around Horseshoe Crab Cove and included all eight Darn Yarner dwellings. It took up the length of a picnic table that stood just inside the barn.

The barn's chandeliers were draped with greenery and wildflowers, and the center of each long rustic table was a profusion of greens, flowers, and seashells. Salters Catering had brought in special colorful dishware and festive linens in bright shades of blues, greens, and yellows. As guests mingled sipping drinks, the Salters crew passed hot and cold appetizers. Several tables held an assortments of local cheeses, breads, and antipasto. After much deliberation, the menu had wound up "eclectic," as Lucy described it. Salters had set up four stations, one vegetarian—portabella and bean burgers, roasted vegetable kabobs and salads, a second with their signature barbecue with chicken, pulled pork, sausages, hamburgers, and hot dogs, the third, summer pasta dishes, and the last, seafood kabobs and a huge bowl of lobster salad.

Aisha and Billy wandered off, leaving Karen at the barn door, gazing around, marveling how it had all come together. Lynn and Harriet strolled up, dodging servers who were setting up the buffets.

Harriet slipped her arm around her friend's shoulder, whispering, "How you holding up?"

"You saw, then."

Harriet nodded. Lynn stepped away, allowing the close friends time to check in.

"I'm fine. Weirdness passed." She leaned forward to call Lynn closer. "How are the Caseys doing in their new home?"

"We're loving it. You'll have to come see. We're planning a housewarming soon."

Karen grinned as she gestured at the crowd. "Be careful or you'll have the whole town. It's really hard around here to know when to cut off the guest list."

"This is beyond incredible," Lynn said.

"The crowd or this?" Harriet asked, waving toward the barn's interior.

"Everything. Your moms, this town, and how much they're loved and how much they've done for so many people."

Karen laughed. "Including tripling the population. Look at all their offspring. I guess they didn't get the memo about birth control."

"Well, their offspring have outdone themselves today," Lynn said.

"We did go a little crazy, didn't we?" Harriet said. "Not like me at all."

"We had to find some way for all our filthy-rich brothers to contribute," Karen said, glad to be in the company of women and away from the awkwardness of her encounter with Rich and Sara. "In fact, here come two of the deep pockets now."

Two of her tall, dark-haired brothers approached, beers in hand. "Hey, ladies," Jonas Miller said, his older brother, Rex Junior, beside him. "Great party."

"Says two of our sponsors. This is what the big bucks gets you," Karen said.

Rex hugged her. "Every penny well spent. This place is amazing, isn't it? Forget the big city. I should move back and work from here."

"Wouldn't you find it a little tame?" Karen asked, gazing up at him.

Rex shrugged, his gesture so like their father's. "Maybe, but it might be worth a try. Hey, who's that blonde hanging all over Coop Merrick?"

Karen followed his gaze and spied Coop and Kiki Bloom talking with Tim and Gail. Truth be told, Coop looked slightly uneasy. "That's Morgan's Fire's new resident vet."

Rex turned to Harriet. "What about your husband? I thought that's what brought him back east?"

Karen frowned, poking her brother. "Aren't you forgetting my best friend? She's the one who lured him away from Saguaro Valley."

Harriet smiled, ignoring her friend. "Kyle is the town vet and is loving it, but he's super busy. Richard felt they needed a full-time person out here."

"Gus thinks he's following his brother's and Spark's model for Valley Stables." Lynn said. She referred to Ben Morgan, Richard's older brother, who lived in Arizona and had recently started a thoroughbred farm with his college friend, Spark Foster.

Harriet laughed. "It's called doing things as big as possible when you have the means to do it."

Karen elbowed her brother. "So is the lovely Dr. Bloom the reason for your sudden interest in moving back home?"

Rex grinned. "I'm with Daphne, remember?"

"Uh-huh."

"How are things in Saguaro?" Lynn asked Jonas, an engineer, who had recently relocated to the Southwest and was working for one of Spark Foster's alternative energy companies.

"Goin' great," he said. "I've barely spent any time in the Valley, though, as I'm all over the West Coast."

A bell rang, and eyes turned to find Richard Morgan standing on a bench, Lucy by his side. "Good evening, folks! Thrilled to have everyone here. This isn't my party, but the work of this lady right here and all the other Darn Yarn-ettes, or our honorees' amazing kids. Lucy, would you like to say a few words?"

Lucy smiled, gazing toward the table where her mother and her fellow Yarners sat. "Only that this has truly been a labor of love for these eight extraordinary women, and now, dinner's up! Enjoy, everyone!"

Richard hopped off the bench and extended his hand to his wife, helping her down and hugging her.

Will I ever find love like that? Karen mused, watching them. It was the same thought she had when she watched her parents and so many other couples in town. *When will it be my time?* She linked arms with Harriet and headed inside to find a seat.

Karen sat with Harriet and Kyle and a few of her friends and siblings. She tried unsuccessfully to keep her attention on the table's conversation and not on the couple sitting across the room. At one point, she glanced over and met Rich's eyes. He looked sad as he held her gaze. The moment ended when Sara noticed where his attention lay and called him back. "Okay, sis?" Jonas asked, bringing her back. "It's almost time for our performance, right?"

Karen nodded. "Once everyone has their dessert."

After plates were cleared, the Salters crew invited people to view the cake one last time before it was sliced. As pieces of cake were served, diners hopped up with plates to get ice cream, coffee, and tea from the dessert buffet. When everyone was settled back down, Lucy stood and rang a bell. As the barn grew silent, she said, "Calling all Yarn-ettes!"

From around the room, the offspring of Helen, Faith, Rosa, Mavis, Hope, and Belle stood up and came to the far end of the barn, where Richard had had a small temporary stage built. The only children not in attendance were Cora, Grace Straley's daughter, who lived and worked in Scotland Dand had not been able to get away, and Helen's youngest, Hazel, who was leading a tour group in New Zealand. The trip had been booked a year earlier by her company, Parkland Adventures.

When the group was assembled, Sandy nodded to the band, and they began playing the melody of "You Got a Friend in Me," to which the songsters had written new lyrics. Their version with eight verses managed to include all eight Darn Yarners. After that, they sang a silly irreverent version of Garth Brooks's "Friends in Low Places," weaving town lore and more anecdotes about the honorees. They completed their song to thunderous applause and calls for the Yarners.

All eight women came to the stage and were each presented with a beautifully wrapped little box. They opened them to find silver bangle bracelets engraved with all eight names and "40 Years of Friendship." Clara, Helen's daughter, had contracted a silversmith friend to design them specially for the event. There wasn't a dry eye among the grateful honorees, who hugged each other, children, and friends as the crowd called, "Speech, speech!"

The group declined to speak and slowly dispersed with grateful waves and blowing of kisses. As Yarners and their offspring stepped off the stage, Rich came up beside Karen. "I'd really like to see you sometime. Could we?" he whispered.

Without looking at him, she replied, "Probably not a good idea. Excuse me."

She hurried out of the barn, circling around to the deluxe porta-john bathrooms Richard had ordered. Once inside, she locked the door and sat on the closed toilet seat, hands covering her face. *Maybe I can stay here all night*, she mused, as Harriet knocked on the door.

"Come on out, sweetie. They left, so the coast is clear."

"What do you mean, they left?" Karen opened the porta-john door and stepped out.

"Disappeared right after we sang."

"So much for wanting to talk. Come on, let's go back inside. I'm ready to drink too much and dance all night."

Harriet grinned, the moonlight shining on her kind, lovely face. "That's the spirit!"

CHAPTER 22

Rich dropped Sara at her house. Feigning illness, Sara had begged him to stay with her. He made sure she was settled in, but declined to stay as it was obvious the only reason she had begged to leave was to get him as far away from Karen as possible. They had had a number of oblique conversations over the last month. Two nights earlier, he had suggested that maybe their original breakup had been for the best. The explosion that followed revealed a side of Sara he'd never seen before. It was time to end things once and for all. He had no problem making difficult decisive moves in business, so why couldn't he do it here? He didn't love her and really hadn't ever. Their relationship had been convenient and easy once, but that was no longer enough. He wanted more. He wanted Karen.

As he pulled into his driveway, he paused, then said, "Screw it," backed up, and sped up to the main road leading to Morgan's Fire. When he returned to the reception, he spied Karen dancing with Kevin Averill, son of Hank, who owned the general store in town. Strong and muscular, his brown hair tousled, Kevin had always been what people called slow. He did odd jobs around town and was loved by all. Rich smiled as he watched them.

Tim Miller sidled up to stand beside him. "That's my sister for you. Poor Kev doesn't know what hit him."

Rich laughed. "Probably not, but she looks like she's having fun."

"That's what shots of Jack Daniels and beer chasers looks like."

"Uh-oh, really?"

"She's on a tear for some reason. My brothers and I may need to haul her out of here soon."

The music stopped and the two watched as Karen leaned against her dance partner. As the band started playing Lonestar's "Amazed," Rich patted Tim's shoulder. "Lemme get in one dance before you carry her off."

As he headed across the dance floor, Tim called, "You've been warned!"

Rich caught Karen as she stumbled back out of Kevin's grasp. "Mind if I cut in?"

A huge shiteater grin on his face, Kevin waved his hand as he stepped aside. "Be my guest. She's a wild one."

Arm around her waist, Rich drew her close.

Karen's eyes registered surprise. "Oh, you're back."

"Yup," he said, "And I've got you, babe."

"Where's Sara?"

"Took her home," he whispered as his lips brushed her neck.

"And?" she asked, eyes slightly glazed as she stared into his.

"And I've missed you."

"Not sure what that means," she said as she pressed against him, his arousal caressing her. "Something seems to be working. Is it?"

Rich grinned, kissing her forehead. "Far as I know. Haven't taken it for a test drive."

"What about the fair Sara?"

"We don't have that kind of relationship. Not anymore."

"Oh?" She swiveled her hips against him. "What kind *do* you have?"

"Not this kind. We're just friends."

"Does she know that?"

"No, but I'm going to tell her."

"When?"

"Soon."

"Friends? Is that what we are?" she asked, eyes dreamy as she looked up.

Rich shrugged. "Hell if I know."

"Let's find out." Karen took his hand and led him off the dance floor.

Rich knew he should stop her—*not fair in her condition*—but every part of him ached for her. He followed her out of the barn. "Hey, babe, where are we going?"

"You'll see!"

"Will you look at that," Rex Miller said as he and Faith watched Karen drag Rich away.

"That's trouble. That's what that is," she said, shaking her head. "Our baby's definitely had too much to drink."

He laughed. "Maybe it's smartened her up."

"Doubtful. Should we send one of her brothers after them?"

"Absolutely not!" he said, taking her hand. "Come on, Mama, let's dance. Let the kids take care of themselves."

KAREN DRAGGED HIM AROUND THE SIDE OF THE BARN PAST THE PORTA-johns to the recently erected greenhouses. There were canvas tarps on the back ends draped over boarded sides that were waiting for the glass delivery. When she reached the far end, she pulled him into the shadows. "This is as good a place as any," she whispered, pulling him to her. "Are you ready to find out what kind of relationship *we* have?"

He held her at arm's length. "Not sure this is the best time or place."

"Why not?" she asked, her hips moving closer, caressing and insistent.

"Because you've had too much to drink and I've been kind of a jerk."

Karen reached up, arms circling his neck. "I'm just fine, thank you and I forgive you. Kiss me, please."

In reply, he captured her full luscious lips in a deep kiss, lots of tongue, his hands moving from her waist to stroke and tease her round, perfect breasts. He could feel her nipples grow hard, and he groaned. "You know I might not be able to stop this if we keep going."

"Who said anything about stopping," she murmured, returning his kisses. Her hands moved down to stroke him. Suddenly, she pulled back, gazing up at him. "Oh... I didn't ask. Is this okay?"

"More than okay," he said, hands moving under her sweater to cup her breasts, fingers flicking back her lacy bra.

"No, I mean after your surgery. Are you still healing? Is it safe?"

"According to Dr. Carina, if I'm careful, sex is good for my recovery."

"Well, if it's doctor's orders, then who am I to object?" Karen arched her back, offering herself to him. "That's better." She unzipped his pants, released his cock, and began a rhythmic stroking. Rich's hands moved to her waist, and he fumbled. "Here, allow me," she said, unzipping her jeans and dropping them and her panties to the ground.

He slipped fingers between her legs, her slick wet center beckoning him as her found her clit and sent her into orbit.

"Oh...oh...oh," she moaned, writhing under his touch as he brought her to climax.

"Want more?" he whispered huskily.

"You inside me. Now!"

Rich reached in his pocket and extracted a condom from his wallet. It was old, but he always kept one just in case. *Hope it's still safe,* he thought as he slipped it on, wondering if he could hold on much longer. She was literally driving him crazy. He reached down and grabbed her round, beautiful ass, lifting her to wrap her legs around him. As they pressed back against the greenhouse wall, he plunged into her warm sweet depths as Karen met him, sighing.

Their perfect synchrony matched the strands of music that drifted over the night as they took each other to a smashing simultaneous climax. As Karen collapsed against his shoulder, he kissed her neck, then found her lips. "Baby, that was amazing."

"Mm," she murmured, almost purring as she curled up in his arms.

After a few minutes, Rich's legs began to shake. Reluctantly, he put her down. "Sorry, guess I'm still a little weak."

"Not from where I'm standing," she said, standing on tiptoes to kiss him. "You're perfect."

No I'm not, he thought. *I'm a royal shit to have taken advantage of her in this way.*

He bent to retrieve their clothes. "We should get back."

Still tipsy, Karen looked around, appearing confused as he handed her clothes to her.

After they dressed, he took her hand. "Come on, baby. Let's get you home."

Karen had come with her brother, Brick and his wife, Susie. When she and Rich rounded the side of the barn, they spied the couple near the door. "There you are," Brick called. "Gotta get back for our sitter. We almost left without you." His gaze traveled over his sister, and he asked, "Are you okay?"

"Never better," she said dreamily, turning to give Rich a long, lingering kiss before stumbling along beside the couple.

Rich watched them go, then gazed around, spying his father and Lucy at one of the nearby tables. He headed over and placed a hand on his father's shoulder. "Hey, Dad, I'm gonna take off. Great party, Lucy. The Yarners got their due."

Lucy smiled up at him. "I hope so. They sure deserve it."

Rich bent to kiss her cheek, thinking as he had many times how lucky his father was, how lucky they all were, to have Lucy in their lives. "Night," he said as he turned away.

Richard looked at his wife. "He seem okay to you?"

"Maybe a little tired?" she said.

"I'll check in with him in the morning."

CHAPTER 23

Rich slept late, nursing a headache. He'd only had a couple of beers at the Darn Yarner celebration, but during the toasts, he'd downed two glasses of champagne. Champagne always gave him a headache. As he lay staring at the bedroom's ceiling rafters, someone rang the front doorbell. A minute later, the person began knocking more and more insistently. He hopped up and went to the hall window facing the driveway. Sara's car was parked next to his BMW.

"Shit," he muttered, glad he had refused her request for a key several weeks earlier.

Poking his head out the window, he called, "Hold on. Be right down."

The pounding stopped. He grabbed a bathrobe and headed down. When he opened the door, she stormed past, not even glancing at him. Rich followed her into the sunroom, where she was pacing, arms flailing out at her sides.

"Sara, what's going on?"

"I'm pissed! That's what's going on. Guess who was the talk of my early morning class?"

"I haven't the faintest idea," he said, reasonably certain of what was to come next. *Damn the town gossip hotline!*

"You, that's who! You and your white-hot dance number with your little farm girl! Right in the middle of downward dogs, I hear women giggling about your 'dirty dance moves' and how you disappeared into the night *together* right after!"

"Sara, Karen and I are friends. You and I, are too, for that matter."

"Bullshit!"

For a devoted yoga practitioner, she's not very serene, he mused, wondering what he could say to promote calmness. "Listen, Sara, I'm not sure what you heard."

She began pacing again. "Does it matter? You went back to be with her, that's all I need to know. I've been trying so hard this past month. To care for you, to show my love in any way I can. I don't deserve to be humiliated this way!"

"No one's humiliated you," he said quietly. "As I've told you a bunch of times, you and I not back together, but I'm happy to be your friend. Should we talk about things and where we stand?"

She plopped down on a wicker settee. "Fine! Good. Talk."

"Why don't I throw on some clothes. There's coffee brewed. Help yourself."

"You know damn well I don't drink coffee." She stayed seated, but waved her hand dismissively. "Go, I'll wait here."

Rich headed upstairs and pulled on jeans and a faded HCC T-shirt, the latter depicting the town mascot, a large brown horseshoe crab. Steeling himself, he went down, poured a mug of coffee, and came to sit across from her on one of the sunporch's wicker chairs. "Can I get you tea or anything? Water?"

She shook her head. "No, thanks."

"Sara, I'm really sorry if you felt humiliated. This is my fault for not being clearer about you and me." He met her brown eyes. Sara opened her mouth to speak, but then stayed silent. "I like you. I always have, but I don't love you. I'm sorry, because you're a lovely person who deserves a loving partner. He's just not me."

"You only say that because you're involved with Karen Miller."

"That's not true."

"Well, you're lying about you just being friends."

"You may be right. You are right, but she has nothing to do with you and me. We broke up long before anything started with Karen."

"So you admit there is a Karen-and-you that's more than friends."

He nodded. "Yes."

"Do you love her?"

Do I? he mused. *If I do, I'm certainly not going to say it now. Not until I say something to Karen.* "I guess I'll discover that if we become more involved."

"But what about you and me? The past month?"

"Friends hanging on hoping for more?"

"Not from my end," she said quietly, all the fight knocked out of her.

"I'm sorry. I really am."

Sara stood grabbing her small backpack from the floor. "Me too. Goodbye, Rich. Good luck."

Not waiting for his reply, she hurried out, closing the front door quietly behind her.

"Geez," he said aloud. "What the hell am I doing?"

After a few minutes' deliberation, he grabbed his cell phone and punched in Karen's number. She answered with a friendly "Hey, you."

Rich swallowed and asked, "How are you?"

"Great, fine. Maybe slightly hungover. I remember the end of the night, though," she drawled in a flirty, come-hither voice. "I'm in the barn. Let me step outside, out of my brother's earshot."

"Listen, Karen. I'm really sorry about that."

"What do you mean?"

"I took advantage of you when you'd had too much to drink."

"No, you didn't. I wanted it as much as you."

"Last night never should have happened."

"What?"

"Sara's just been here. Apparently, our dance was the hot topic in yoga class this morning."

"Sara, Sara, always Sara! Screw you, Rich Morgan!" With that, she clicked off.

When he redialed, her phone went straight to voicemail.

"Perfect," he said, slamming his coffee mug into the sink just as his phone rang again.

Assuming it was Karen, he didn't look at caller ID as he said, "Oh, so glad you called back."

"Son, is that you?" Richard Morgan said.

"Oh, Dad, sorry. I was waiting for a...never mind. How are you?"

"Doin' fine. Just checkin' if you're on your way?"

"Excuse me?"

"We're meeting with Zeke, Gail, and your brother this morning, remember? The ad firm comes Monday morning? We wanted to brainstorm a bit?"

"Geez, Dad, I'm sorry. I completely lost track of time. Be there in twenty minutes."

"We'll be in the tasting barn. Everything okay?"

"Fine, perfect. See you soon." Rich clicked off shaking his head. *Could this morning get any worse?*

CHAPTER 24

The moment she spied her friend, Harriet sensed trouble. The scowl on her pretty face and the abrupt way she was handling the horses were so unlike her. "Hey, morning! Am I late?"

Karen forced a smile. "Not at all. Right on time."

"Then what's going on?"

"Nothing." Karen stroked Brandi's muzzle, resting against her strong shoulder.

Hands on hips, Harriet gave her a look. "Karen, we've been best friends for thirty-five years."

"Has it been that long? You only moved to town about twenty-five years ago, right?"

"Ha-ha. Our moms were summer buddies since before we were born." Harriet shook her head. "But never mind that. You know what I mean. You kept me sane through the horror show of Hill House and the nightmare of Louis. You know me, and I know you. Now what's wrong?"

It was true. The friends had been through so much over the years. All Karen's romances and broken engagements, Harriet's father's drunken rages and her grandmother's craziness. Karen had been there when Louis disappeared with Harriet's inheritance and broke her heart.

"If I tell you, will you just listen and not try to fix it?"

"Okay." Harriet mounted Rebel, Faith Miller's horse. Karen's mother rarely rode anymore. The beautiful chestnut Morgan was among the gentlest of the Land's End stable horses.

"Let's ride awhile till I cool down."

"How you doing, son?" Richard asked, as they headed into the winery's tasting barn. Richard had been waiting for him, leaning against one of the farm trucks.

"I thought you'd already be inside?"

"Not without my main man." Richard paused at the barn door and placed a hand on Rich's shoulder.

"Dad, I appreciate your concern, but I'm fine."

"Could've fooled me."

"I don't want to talk about it. Please drop it, okay?" His father had been his best friend for as long as Rich could remember. He loved him and trusted him. He also knew that talking things through with him would help, but not at this moment. "Come on, the others are waiting."

"Okay, but I'm here for you. You know that, right?"

Rich gave him a tired smile. "I do, and I'm grateful. Later, okay?"

"You bet," his father said, following him into the barn. "Morning, team!" he called, greeting Wolfie, Zeke, and Cara, Zeke's assistant and apprentice.

Wolfie stood and made room for his father next to Zeke. He was the vineyard manager, but his father was in charge. No matter how much Richard endeavored to step back, his offspring always deferred to him, even Rich.

"Morning, guys," Wolfie said. "You okay, brother? You look a little green around the gills." Behind Rich, his father shook his head, and Wolfie got the message. "Guess we're all a little green after the Darn Yarner extravaganza. There's coffee and muffins over there if you want them."

Rich grabbed a blueberry muffin and a bottle of water from the counter and came to sit next to his youngest brother. "It's looking great in here," he said.

"We're trying," Wolfie said. "Now, about this Aaron Parker."

"Where's Gail?" Rich asked. "She should be here for this."

"Running late. She should be here soon," Richard said.

As if on cue, the door opened, and Gail Morgan Miller stepped in.

"Morning, princess," her father said.

Gail rolled her eyes at her father before taking a seat beside Cara. "Ignore him. Still thinks I'm five years old."

Cara smiled. "My dad does the same thing." Roughly the same age as her manager, they were by far the youngest in the room. Athletic and strong, Cara wore her blonde hair tied in a long braid. Zeke's apprentice had a handsome beauty that shone best in her blue eyes. When hired, she had made it very clear that this was a "temporary gig." Ambitious and smart, she wanted to learn from Zeke, then move on to a vintner position of her own.

"Sorry I'm late. Shall we get started?" Gail asked, opening a folder as she gazed around the table. "Aaron Parker is the best of the best. If he's willing to take us on, we'll be beyond lucky."

"All due respect," Zeke said, "it may be a little soon."

Gail gazed over at the short, burly vintner with his bushy gray hair and piercing dark eyes. Still strong as an ox, it was hard to believe he was in his late seventies. "You may be right, Zeke, but Aaron contacted us, and I don't think we can refuse to at least meet with him and see what he has to say."

"Agreed," her father said.

"We're not committing to anything," Rich said. "And we have lots of other options." He opened his briefcase. "So, Gail, what's our strategy going to be?"

~

"I am so dumb," Karen said as the friends stood together at the overlook at the mouth of the harbor. The horses grazed nearby in the grassy area, and a warm breeze blew off the water. "I hate being the dumb girl."

"You're not dumb. Maybe a little confused and hurt? Not that it will make you feel any better, but I bet he is too."

"No, it doesn't. Besides, he has Sara to comfort him."

"You don't know that."

"But I do."

"Did he say as much?" Harriet asked.

"Didn't have to. All I know is that one of the most passionate nights of my life meant nothing to him."

"I'm sure that's not true."

"Well then, why did he say it never should have happened?"

"I don't know him well, but Rich has always impressed me as the steadiest Morgan. Kind, calm, and unflappable. Maybe the other night surprised him?"

"You'd never know it. He was all in, I can tell you. At least from what I remember."

Harriet smiled, putting her arm around Karen's waist. "Could it be that he's a gentleman and he's giving you both some space to figure things out?"

Karen chuckled, pushing her away. "Now I've heard everything! Let's just forget about Rich and enjoy this beautiful day."

"Lead the way, dearie!" Harriet said as they turned back to their horses.

CHAPTER 25

After their ride, Harriet and Karen had lunch at the Café. As they parted company, Harriet said, "Maybe give him a chance and talk when you feel better?"

"No, no, and no," Karen said. "I've cut those strings. Now I've got to scoot. Andy's been texting for the past hour to see when I'm coming in."

As Karen headed down Main Street to the building across from Laura's Garden, her phone pinged. Yet another message from Rich. She hit delete.

"Hi, Karen!" Pam called as she stepped into the foyer. Pam Morgan and another therapist shared the building with Andy's accounting business.

"Hey," she said, pausing. She really liked all the Morgan siblings, but she felt awkward today after the falling-out with Rich.

"How's things?" Pam asked, coming to greet her.

"Great, never better," she lied, forcing a smile.

"You pulled it off, didn't you?"

"Excuse me?"

"The Darn Yarners party. It was so much fun."

Karen shook herself back to reality. "Yes, it was. The moms had a ball. And it wasn't just their kids who pulled it off. Look at all you did, and your dad. He really knows how to throw a party."

Pam smiled, a warm, gentle smile like her oldest brother's. "He loves nothing better."

"Speaking of parties, how's yours coming along? Only a few weeks now, right?"

Pam blanched. "Don't remind me. We wanted small and low-key, but that was wishful thinking."

Karen laughed. "What about the West Coast contingent? Are a lot of them coming?"

Pam shrugged, raising her hands. "Our uncle and aunt, maybe one or two of the cousins. Knowing them, at the last minute, Spark Foster could fly in the whole ranch."

"Very cool having a private jet."

"Or jets, I understand."

"Why doesn't your dad have one?"

"Don't give him any ideas!"

"Does Sandy's family have a lot of people coming?"

Pam nodded. "You have no idea! Every one of Rosa's siblings has a big family."

"Gonna be fun."

"Says you." The door opened, and a freckle-faced teenager with baggy pants and inverted baseball cap opened the front door. "Hi, Jimmy, go on back. I'll be right there." Pam turned back to Karen, patting her arm. "You and my brother really know how to heat up the dance floor," she whispered. "So glad for you!"

As Rich's sister disappeared, Karen groaned, heading back to the office. *You wouldn't be glad if you knew what was really going on.*

POST-OP APPOINTMENT OVER, RICH EXITED THE MEDICAL BUILDING. As he stepped into the sun, he thought back to the day he ran into Karen six weeks earlier. She had been so warm and solicitous, a friend when he'd really needed one. *Boy, did I screw that up*, he mused, headed for his car.

Everything looked good, according Dr. Carina, although he had raised a surprised eyebrow when Rich told him that he'd had sex and everything worked just fine. "We usually give the okay on sexual relations at this appointment," the doctor said, "but hey, if you're ahead of the game in that department, I'm glad for you. Do take it easy, though."

"No worries there," Rich had assured him. *In fact, at this rate, I may be celibate forever!* He was about to start the BMW when he changed his mind. "What have I got to lose?" he said aloud, stepping out and heading down the street.

He passed several people he knew as he walked the short distance to Andy Roby's office. He waved but didn't stop to chat. He took the porch steps two at a time, praying his sister would be with a client. He could hear Andy's voice at the far end of the hall as he stepped into the foyer. He knew the accountant, with whom he had had several conversations about work for Morgan Enterprises. So far, all their accounting was handled by a firm in Maine, but he and his father had been considering moving things to town.

When he stepped into the outer office, Andy waved from his private office. Rich returned the wave, then turned to spy Karen on the floor, sorting papers. When she looked up and spotted him, she frowned. "Are you here to see Andy?"

"No." She looked especially pretty in a sleeveless white linen top and tan capris. Barefoot, she'd tossed her sandals willy-nilly next to her chair and tied her hair back with tortoiseshell clips. *How can I turn this around?* he thought, trying to stay calm.

"Do you want to make an appointment?"

"No, I want to talk to you. Please."

"No."

"Just five minutes, please, Karen."

Abruptly, she stood. Not bothering with her sandals, she marched out of the office toward the front door. Rich followed, hoping this meant she would hear him out. No such luck.

Karen stepped onto the porch, eyes blazing, arms akimbo.

"Thanks for this," he said.

She raised her hand. "There is no 'this.' Now go. I don't make scenes at my place of work, but I don't want to talk to you in any case."

He reached out, but she stepped back. "I am so sorry, Karen."

Her eyes softened, but her mouth remained set, her expression resolute. "I know you are, but I have nothing to say to you right now. Please go."

"But—"

"Now."

The door opened behind them, and a young man stepped out, Rich's sister right behind him. As she said, "Bye, Scott," Pam gazed at her brother, eyes questioning.

Karen took the opportunity to quickly step around her and disappear inside, leaving brother and sister standing on either side of the door. "Everything okay?" she asked.

Rich rolled his eyes. "Don't ask. See you, sis."

Before she could ask further, he turned and walked away.

CHAPTER 26

"Not that it's my business," Pam said, "but does anyone know what's up with Rich and Karen?" She had stopped by to discuss wedding plans with Lucy and Weezie and was now enjoying a late-afternoon glass of wine on the front porch with her sister, father, and Lucy. "This is really good wine, by the way. Can we make this kind here?"

Richard laughed. "I doubt it, but we can check with our vintner. And to answer your other question, I think there may be some tension in that relationship."

"Why? What happened?"

"Our sainted brother has been juggling two women, and one of them has had enough."

"Now that may not be entirely fair, pumpkin," their father said.

Weezie shook her head, waving her empty beer bottle in the air. "What would you know? You're a man."

Lucy set down her wine. "Your father may be right here. I mean, Sara Gregson's a lovely person, but it did seem to us that she pushed her way back into your brother's life at a vulnerable time for him."

"Doesn't mean he couldn't have pushed her right back out," Weezie said.

Pam grinned. "Are talking about the same brother? Never-Make-Waves Rich?"

"Now that's *really* not fair!" Richard said. "Rich can be as forceful and dynamic as the next man."

"In business, Dad," Pam said. "Affairs of the heart might be a bit different. I love him, but when have you known him to be dynamic in love? Every girlfriend he's ever been with has worn the pants in the relationship, or at least played the leading role."

"That's because he's kind and considerate," Lucy said quietly. "Those are wonderful qualities."

Pam shrugged. "Whatever. I did feel sorry for him today. He came to the office and Karen pretty much told him to get lost."

"Gee, poor guy. Maybe I should pop over, see how he's doing," Richard said. "Or call and see if he wants to come to dinner? I'm sure Callie made plenty."

"That may not be necessary," Lucy said, gazing up the driveway as the gray BMW headed their way.

Richard stood up, then sat. "Good, great. Now, no one say a thing, okay?"

"Yeah, right," Weezie said, heading for the door. "I'm getting another beer. Anyone want something?"

The group ignored her, all eyes on Rich as he parked and hopped out.

"Evening, son!" Richard called. "I hope you're here for dinner?"

Rich smiled. "Only if there's enough." He turned to Pam. "What are you doing here?"

"Wedding stuff."

Weezie stepped back on the porch and handed him a beer.

"Thanks, sis."

"So what's new?" Richard asked as Rich took the seat next to him.

"I wanted to stop by and tell you I'm heading to Maine for a couple of days."

"When?" Richard asked.

"Early tomorrow morning."

"Want company son?"

"No, thanks, Dad. I need some peace and quiet to sort things through. I'm staying with Aunt Cherie. Called her earlier. I'll meet with the accountants, make the rounds to our suppliers, and visit with Cherie."

"I wish I could come with you," Pam said.

Rich gave her a look, then gazed around at his family. "I'm sure you filled them in, didn't you?"

"No," she said. "I mean... I did ask... I wondered about you and Karen today."

Rich shrugged. "She hates me. I don't blame her a bit." He proceeded to summarize the events of recent days, omitting the details of their white-hot sex.

At the end of his story, Pam said, "Sounds like a cooling-off period might help?"

"I doubt it," her brother said, the picture of dejection, his straight hair falling across his forehead as he bent over, elbows on knees, beer set on the porch floor.

"I think Pam's right," Weezie said. "I don't know her that well, but it seems like Karen's a bit of a hothead. She'll probably calm down. What do you think, Lucy? Isn't she like your sister's best friend?"

Lucy nodded. "And she's been a wonderful friend to Harriet. Not a mean bone in her body. She's a strong, seemingly confident woman, but there's a sensitive soul underneath the façade."

"Sure is," Rich said. "And I pretty much trampled all over it."

The group sat in silence for a few minutes, sipping drinks until Callie popped her head out. "Dinner's ready whenever you are," she said softly. "No hurry, though."

"WHAT'S GOTTEN INTO HER?" REX MILLER SAID, REFERRING TO HIS daughter, who had stormed into the house and stomped upstairs without a word to either of them.

Faith shrugged. "Darned if I know, but if I had to guess, it has something to do with Rich Morgan. She's crazy about him, you know."

"I should hope so after their dancing at your party."

Faith stepped into the hallway and called up, "Dinner in five minutes!" When she returned, she said, "And if you know what's good for you, you'll leave it alone. Don't pry."

Rex chuckled. "Like you won't, honey?"

"Humph," she said, reaching into the oven with mitted hands to bring out the roast chicken. It was one of her daughter's favorite meals, and she knew from the village grapevine that it had been a rough day for her baby.

A few minutes later, the baby appeared, freshly showered and wearing gray sweatpants and a sleeveless tee. "Hey, Punky," her father said.

Karen poured herself an iced tea and sat down. She gave him a tired smile. 'Hey, Dad."

"Tough day?" he asked, ignoring his wife, who was shaking her head behind Karen.

"I've had better."

"Anything we can help with?"

Karen reached over and patted his hand. "I'm fine, really. Just tired of talking about it."

"You gotta talk," Faith said, setting a plate of chicken, potato salad, and green beans in front of her.

"Not today, I don't."

"Nothing was ever settled by silence," her mother continued, completely ignoring her earlier resolve not to pry.

"Mom, Dad, listen. I know you mean well and I love you for it, but I just don't want to talk about Rich. I'm sick of the whole stupid subject." She took a bite of chicken and closed her eyes. "Mm, that's great."

They ate in silence for several minutes, enjoying the succulent chicken. Village lore had it that no one made roast chicken like Faith Miller. Finally, Faith said, "You know, honey, you've always been in the driver's seat when it comes to men."

"What's that supposed to mean?"

"It's been easy for you. Love 'em, have some fun, then move on. You've never gotten too attached."

"Not true!"

"Honey, how many times have you been engaged, or about to be?"

"That has no relevance here."

"They've all been crazy about you. Your dad and I have watched man after man fall head over heels, only to have his heart broken. What's different here is that you really fell for this one in a way you never have before."

"And how would you know?" All the fight knocked out of her, Karen gazed across the table.

"I'm your mother, and mothers know these things."

"Not this time, Mom. I barely know Rich, and it's probably better to keep it that way."

"We don't keep hospital vigils for people we barely know. You're in love with him, honey. Don't you want to see where it leads?"

Rex looked from mother to daughter. "Great meal, isn't it, Punky?"

The two women regarded him as if he'd lost his mind, then Karen said, "I've seen where it leads, and it's over."

"All right, honey, no more nagging. I've got apple crisp for dessert."

"I'm full. Thanks, Mom." She stood and took her plate to the sink.

"Oh, Punky, I forgot to mention the backhoe. Your brother says something's jammed in the hydraulics."

"Well, tell him to fix it or call Eastlands."

"It's just something simple. Brick said you've worked on it before."

Karen stacked plates in the dishwasher, then said, "Fine. It's too dark now, but I'll take a look first thing. Not that I don't have a million other things to do tomorrow."

Her parents exchanged looks, and Faith said, "Sure you don't want to take some apple crisp up with you?"

"No thanks. I'm beat. Night."

CHAPTER 27

Rich headed out of town at first light, glad to put some distance between him and Horseshoe Crab Cove. *At least everyone won't be looking over my shoulder in Maine*, he thought. He tried Karen's cell, but it went to voicemail. He left a message. "Hey, it's me. Not going to bother you anymore. Just wanted you to know I'm going out of town for a few days. I still hold out hope that we can talk sometime when I get back. Hope you have a great day." As he clicked off, Rich wondered if she'd even bother to listen or just hit Delete.

Karen did listen, then hit Delete and threw her cell phone across the barn floor as she stowed her toolbox and hopped in her truck to head out to the north field where the jammed backhoe stood waiting for her.

As she scooched under the front of the backhoe dragging her toolbox, she thought back to the day she'd met Rich after his appointment, when he'd just heard the news about his cancer. There was a vulnerability about the handsome Morgan son that had touched her heart as no man ever had. A softness, like her own father, an open heart that was scarred and needed nurturing. He had tapped into her best self that day, the compassionate, good-hearted person she wanted to be, yet often found impossible. *What the hell happened to the simplicity of that day? Love, that's what. And love complicates everything!*

She'd been working about a half hour when she managed to find what she thought was the issue. As she worked to free a jammed cylinder, she moved farther and farther under the boom, her body now wedged against metal and the ground. Just as she considered whether this was wise with no one else around, the cylinder broke free and the weight of the boom fell. Karen screamed, then everything went black.

"WHOSE PHONE IS THIS THROWN IN REBEL'S STALL?" REX MILLER asked, holding it up. A couple of their seasonal workers looked up from mucking out the stalls and shrugged.

His son Brick poked his head out of a stall and squinted. "Looks like my dippy sister's. Typical. That's why she has an insurance plan. Has to replace her phone every month for damage or loss. Where is she anyway? This was supposed to be her morning to help out."

"Wasn't she out fixing the backhoe?"

Brick turned and gazed out the barn window. "Her truck's still out there. Figures. We should've called Eastlands. She shouldn't be monkeying around with the big rigs."

"Probably right. Funny it's taken her so long. Maybe I'll ride out and see how she's comin' along."

Rex tucked the cell phone into his pocket and walked toward his truck. As he started it up, his eyes narrowed, and he noticed the odd angle of the backhoe, almost tilted over on its side. Something was wrong. "Brick," he yelled. "Something's happened out there. Bring both the guys and hop in the truck. Now!"

They found Karen unresponsive, her legs pinned under the machine's front end. Miraculously, there was little blood, but her face was gray. Rex knelt beside her, stroking her forehead. "We've gotta get her out of this. Now."

Brick pulled out his cell phone and called 911. "We need an

ambulance at Land's End now!" he cried, then motioned to the two college kids. "Tony, Jazz, we've got to move this thing off her. Dad, we need you to pull her out when we do, okay?"

"You think it's safe?" Rex asked, eyes wild with fear.

"Hell if I know, but she needs medical attention, and she's not gonna get it under there. We three can lift it so you get under her arms and pull gently and steadily."

The next hour was a blur. Faith arrived at the same time as the ambulance. EMTs quickly assessed and determined that Karen should be airlifted to Boston from the Bayport Helipad. As they loaded her into the ambulance, she woke, confused and scared. "What's happened? Mama? Where are they taking me? Why can't I move my legs?"

"Hush, baby. They want to take you to Boston to check you out. I'm coming along for the ride, so let's get going, okay?"

One of the EMTs turned to her. "Sorry, Ms. Miller, not sure if there's room."

Ignoring him, Faith hopped in beside her daughter. "Chip Berube, I've known you since you were in diapers, and I can tell you right now, you're not taking my baby anywhere unless I ride with you. So make room."

"We'll be right behind you honey," Rex said.

"Brick, you stay back, but call your brothers," Faith called. "I don't want Dad driving to Boston alone, and Rex Junior can meet us at the hospital."

"But I—" Brick said.

"No buts, we need you here, honey. We'll call when we get there. Now go!" she said to no one in particular, but everyone moved.

～

"Oh, dear... Sirens," Lucy said as she and her partner Lolly sorted the new shipment of books.

Lolly nodded. "'Cause it's invariably someone we know. How's the wedding planning coming?"

Lucy peeked around stack of boxes, trying to read her friend's expression. Her stepdaughter Pam was marrying Lolly's ex-husband, and the initial stages of their courtship had not gone over well with her hurt, angry friend. "Okay."

Lolly frowned, then waved her hand. "You don't have to look like that. I'm okay with it. I've made my peace and am happy for both of them."

Lucy raised an eyebrow.

"I'm serious. I won't lie, I wish I had someone in my life, what with watching how sickeningly happy you and Richard are and, of course, my ex and Pam. Seems like everyone in this town is pairing up, and I'm shit out of luck. But I'm looking forward to the wedding and seeing my little princess as a flower girl."

"Maisie's going to be adorable. Have you got her dress?"

"Yup. Pam told us the color, but gave us carte blanche to pick out what she liked, or in this case, what Mother wanted. She had photos of every flower girl's dress from every shop in the world on display. Maisie didn't know what hit her." Mavis LaSalle, Lolly's mother, ran an elite and very popular event venue on their extensive property east of town, the Cove Inn and Spa.

"Can't wait to see her. And, dear friend, I'm glad you've made peace with the whole Sandy/Pam thing. There's someone out there for you. I just know there is."

Lolly smiled. "Ever the optimist, aren't you? If I want to find a man, I fear I'm going to have to look a little farther afield."

"Never know... New people are moving in all the time!"

Lolly sighed, stacking several dozen new Mo Willems books on the shelf. "You're lucky, you know. I've never had love like yours, and you've had it twice."

Lucy nodded. "I don't know about Rob... Although I was completely head over heels in the beginning. It's hard to lose your best friend."

"What about Richard, who clearly worships the ground you walk on?"

"Yes, he's the dearest friend and also a wonderful lover and husband, but maybe I'm more realistic now? Less starry-eyed?"

Lolly peered around her book stack and gave Lucy the look. "Have you seen the way you look at him? And he you? Starry-eyed doesn't half cover it. Gaga, over the moon, truly madly, deeply, should I go on?"

Lucy laughed, tossing a ball of packing paper at her. "No!"

"Someone's coming down the hall," Lolly said. "Must be Lynn. We sure need her."

Lynn Casey opened the door, her face ashen. "Hey, sorry I'm late. There's been an accident out at Land's End. Gus went out to help. Richard too."

"Oh my goodness," Lucy said. "Is it Rex or Faith?"

Lynn shook her head. "No, it's Karen. She was working on the backhoe, and it fell on her, pinned her. They've taken her to Boston by helicopter."

"Oh my God," Lolly said, standing up. "Is she going to be okay?"

"Apparently, she has no feeling in her legs. Not sure of anything else."

"Oh, poor Faith and Rex. What can we do?"

"Pray, I guess," Lynn said, coming forward to hug them both.

RICH HAD JUST CROSSED THE BORDER FROM NEW HAMPSHIRE INTO Maine when his stomach lurched and his chest tightened. *I can't do this,* he thought, as he pulled into a parking lot and turned the car around. *I can't go on as if nothing's happened. Not until I have it out with her. No matter what it takes!* A half hour later, as he neared the turn-off for Boston, his cell rang. It was his father.

"Hey, son, there's been an accident out at Land's End. It's Karen. They're airlifting her to Boston. Thought you'd want to know."

Rich asked his father to get the particulars about where she was, then took the Boston exit.

CHAPTER 28

When he arrived on the floor at Mass General, Rich found Faith and Rex Miller in a small waiting area along with Karen's brothers Rex Junior, Tim, and Jonas. Faith's sister Grace sat beside her, holding her hand.

Tim stood and came to greet him. "Hey, man, thanks for coming. How'd you hear?"

"My dad called. I was on my way to Maine. How is she?"

"We're still waiting."

"What the hell happened, Tim?" Rich whispered.

"She was under the backhoe fooling with the hydraulics, and the boom fell on her legs. Pinned her."

"Have they told you anything?"

Tim shook his head. "Nada, zip. We've just gotten our mother to sit down. She's been a wreck."

"Of course she has. What can I do? Can I make a cafeteria run or at least get people waters or coffee?"

"I'm sure they'd...we'd appreciate it. Let me ask."

As Tim stepped away, Frankie Brown walked in and went straight to her dear friend, wrapping her arms around Faith, Rex, and Grace.

"Oh, Frankie," Faith sobbed, her body shaking. "Our baby's hurt real bad."

Tim spoke quietly to his brothers, then returned and said, "I'd just grab a bunch of drinks, maybe some muffins or something. My mom drinks herbal tea. So does Frankie."

As Rich made for the door, Frankie broke away from her friends and called to him, "Hold up, Rich. I'll come with you."

After asking at the nurse's station for directions to the cafeteria, they headed for the elevator. "Did you get where we're going?" she asked him. "This place is huge. I'm surprised I found you at all."

"I think I can find it. Come on."

Five bags and several cardboard drink trays later, they headed back to the elevator. "You were good to come," Frankie said as they waited.

Rich shrugged. "God, I hope she's okay. What the hell was she doing under a friggin' backhoe?"

"That's what she does. Fixes the farm equipment. She's two-thirds of the way through an engineering degree, you know."

"No, I didn't. In fact, what I don't know about Karen could fill a set of encyclopedias."

"But you care about her, don't you?"

He nodded. "Yes."

"Thought as much when I saw you two together at the party."

"Yeah, and then I made a big fat mess of things. She won't even speak to me."

Frankie smiled at him as the elevator's going-up light pinged. "And yet, you're here."

"Pretty dumb, huh?"

"Not from where I'm standing. Come on, before this stuff gets cold."

When they stepped into the lounge, the family was gathered around a tall woman in light-blue scrubs. Faith Miller was asking her, "What does this all mean?"

"There is a fracture at the top of her right tibia. We can repair it, but it means replacing the ball joint to her hip. In essence, what she needs is a total hip replacement."

Faith grasped her husband's hand, eyes riveted on the doctor. "But she told us her legs were numb."

"That's the trauma. It should be temporary. We'll know more in a day or two. We've called for an orthopedic consult as well as neurology."

"So what should we do?" Rex Senior asked.

"Hang tight right now. We'll keep you updated."

"Can we see her?"

"Of course. She should be in her room soon, and a nurse will come for you. Take care, folks."

The group sat in silence as Frankie and Rich offered drinks and snacks. Finally, Rex Junior said, "Let's see what the next few days tell us. My colleague just had a hip replacement at Mercy, and the doc is top-notch. Uses latest technology and techniques."

Jonas nodded. "We should all do some research before she decides anything."

"What about the availability of these guys?" Tim said. "I've heard people wait six months to a year for this kind of surgery."

"I can make some calls," Rich said. "One of my friends from Dartmouth is an orthopedist."

"Oh yes, dear. Thank you," Faith said. "That would be so helpful."

Rich excused himself and went down the hall to phone Jim Muesse, his college roommate. The phone went straight to voicemail, so he left a brief message asking Jim to phone as soon as he could. *Now what do I do?* he thought. *I very much doubt she'll want me trailing along with her family to her room.*

His question was answered sooner than he expected when Frankie strolled down the hall. "Any news?" he said.

"Just that she has a room, 4271. It's private, but only two people can visit at a time. Her mom and dad went up. The guys will wait. I thought I might hang out in the waiting area to feed the troops as they come and go. How about you?"

Rich smiled at her. While he didn't know her well, he'd always liked his Beach Road neighbor. Although she was tall, the fifty-something with curly salt-and-pepper hair and unconventional dress resembled a hobbit. Her home's exterior, with its arched entryway and elaborately carved front door, looked like something straight out of the Middle Earth.

"Happy to help with catering," he said. "Been a while since I pulled an all-nighter. You know...my dad has a trick where he manages to get hospitals to bring in huge, really comfortable recliners for patients' rooms. Not your run-of-the-mill recliners either. Big cushy ones. I could call him and see if he'd be able to work his magic here. What do you think?"

"Genius! Yes give him a call. I'd order two. That way, her parents will get a decent sleep."

Rich grabbed his phone. His father answered on the first ring. "Hey, Dad."

"Hey, son, we've been waiting for your call. Helen's here for dinner. Harriet too. We're all wondering about Karen."

Rich gave him quick summary of what they knew so far, then asked about the recliners. Richard asked for specifics about the room and wing of the hospital, then said, "Consider it done. If they don't materialize in an hour or so, call me back and I'll bring 'em up myself."

"Thanks, Dad," Rich said clicking off.

Frankie shook her head, then met his eye, an astonished expression playing across her normally placid face.

He grinned. "What can I say? Money talks, and Dad has a lot of it."

CHAPTER 29

Late that evening, as Rich and Frankie were cleaning up the lounge, Jonas and Tim flopped side by side in two upholstered chairs, their Aunt Grace on the sofa across from them,

Jim Muesse called.

"Hey, Jim," Rich said, voice low as he set down his trash bag and walked out to the hall.

"Hey, buddy, what's up?" Jim asked, his thick deep voice like a balm to frayed nerves. "You said something about an emergency?"

Rich filled him in, ending with, "So that's where we are."

"If they're replacing her hip, you want Gretchen Cote, at least for a consult. She's the best hip surgeon in the country. She's at Coastal Ortho."

"How would we work that?"

"Sounds like you can't work anything for a few days till you find out if she's stable. I'm in Boston tomorrow. I can give Gretch a call, then stop in and see your Karen. Maybe give Gretchen some sense of what she'd be dealing with?"

"Thanks, man. I'll let the family know. They'll be really grateful."

"No problem, buddy. She must be someone pretty special."

"She is," Rich said, clicking off. *She definitely is.*

~

AFTER HE VISITED WITH KAREN AND HER FAMILY, JIM MUESSE MET RICH in the hospital café. A weary smile played across his open freckled face.

The two friends could not have been more different in appearance. Jim, a stocky, ruddy-cheeked redhead, was a former rugby player who now kept in shape with a daily racquetball game, and Rich, tall, pale-complected, with the slender build of a long-distance runner. They had met their first day at Dartmouth and had roomed together all four years. They still made it a priority to get together regularly for weekend hikes and athletic events.

"Hey, Jimbo," Rich said, giving him a bear hug. "Thanks for coming. I owe you big-time."

"No worries. I had to be in the city anyway. Your girl's a sweetheart."

"I'm afraid she's not my girl at the moment."

"Yeah, what's that about? She didn't even know you were in the hospital."

"Long story for another day."

"She's in a lot of pain, but they're keeping her comfortable and loopy. Sensation hasn't come back to her legs, but that's not unusual. Problem is, I'm guessing Gretchen won't want to do the hip replacement until she stabilizes."

"How long could that be?"

Jim shrugged. "Couple of days, a week, maybe a month? I'll call Gretch in the morning and let her know what I've found. She's usually booked solid a year out, and she almost never gets to Boston. That would be the first step. Get Karen down to Long Bridge to see her."

"Her brother knows someone at Mercy."

Jim shook his head. "There are some great surgeons at Mercy, but if Karen was my daughter, sister, sweetheart, whoever, I wouldn't trust anyone but Gretchen Cote. She's in a class by herself. This is not your run-of-the-mill hip replacement. It's tricky for many reasons."

"Did you tell that to the Millers?"

"Sure did, but I didn't promise anything. Gretchen might just tell me to take a hike till next year."

Rich brushed hair from his forehead, chin resting on his palm. "Thanks, Jim. I owe you one."

"No, you don't, buddy, but let's plan a weekend in the White Mountains soon. What do you say?"

"I say great, but you know you're also welcome at my place. We have great hiking and horseback riding around the farm and village."

"I know... I really have to get down there, don't I?"

The friends chatted a while longer, then hugged as they said their goodbyes. After leaving Jim, Rich headed back to the lounge, where he found everyone except Frankie asleep. Miraculously, five recliners stood side by side along one wall, sofas and chairs pushed aside. Jonas, Tim, and Grace lay sleeping and snoring under thin hospital blankets.

Frankie put a finger to her lips. "Your dad's outdone himself this time. There are two more with eiderdown quilts in Karen's room."

Rich grinned. "That's what he does. Is this one taken?" He pointed to the one nearest the door.

"Has your name written all over it. Let's get some sleep, shall we?"

CHAPTER 30

Karen frowned at her two brothers. "Why didn't someone tell me Rich was in the hospital yesterday?" Her parents had gone down to have breakfast and sent Jonas and Tim in their place.

"Beats me." Jonas gazed around the room, hoping to avoid further interrogation.

Tim came to the bedside and took her hand. "There was a lot going on, sis."

"Bullshit. Why didn't he come up?"

Jonas came to stand on the other side of the bed. "Now, don't get your knickers in a twist. He was being considerate and letting family visit. We can only come two at a time, you know."

"I don't want to see him," she said, withdrawing her hand from Tim's grasp, folding her arms across her chest.

Tim nodded. "There's that too. He didn't want to upset you."

"Then why is he here at all?"

Jonas raised his eyebrow. "Come on, sis, have the drugs you're on addled your brain? He cares about you. A lot."

Karen screwed her face up into a pout. "And why aren't you in Arizona?"

"Was 'sposed to leave last night. I waited till today."

"Not on my account, I hope?"

"Sis, why don't you rest now. Has the doc been in?"

The door behind them opened, and the tall physician from the previous evening stepped in. "Morning, folks. I'm Dr. Faulkner. Beth. I'm an orthopedist. I was on call when they brought you in," she said, smiling as she approached the bedside.

Karen used strong arms to sit up straighter. "What about that doctor with the freckles?"

"That would be Dr. Muesse. He's a specialist your family called in for a consult. I just got off the phone with him."

"Oh?" Tim asked.

Faulkner nodded. Dark circles ringed her blue-gray eyes as she stuffed strands of brown hair back under her surgical cap. "He's a specialist. Unfortunately, he only operates on hands."

"So why did he come?" Karen said.

Faulkner stared at her patient, expression puzzled. "He didn't explain?"

"She was pretty loopy last night," Tim said.

"Dr. Muesse has performed what we might call a medical miracle and gotten you an appointment with Gretchen Cote next week. She's the top hip doc on the East Coast, maybe in the country. She's impossible to get an appointment with unless you're willing to wait five years."

"I think our friend said that Dr. Muesse and Dr. Cote went to medical school together," Jonas said.

"Lucky you."

"What friend?" Karen looked from one to the other. "What are you talking about?"

"Before you three explore that, might I do a quick exam on your sister? Perhaps you'd be so kind as to wait in the hall, gentlemen?"

"I must have been really out of it last night," Karen said as her brothers closed the door behind them

Dr. Faulkner looked up from her chart and smiled. "Probably a good thing. How's the pain this morning? Scale of one to ten?"

"Maybe seven or eight. It comes and goes."

"That's a bit high. Do you want something to make you more comfortable?"

Karen shook her head. "Not if it makes me addled and out of it. I want to be clearheaded. I still can't feel my right leg."

"How about the left?"

In answer, Karen wiggled her toes, then winced as she tried to raise her left leg. "Hurts like hell, but I can move it."

"It's very badly bruised. While nothing's broken on your left side, the bruises are deep."

"And the right?"

"Top of your thigh bone snapped off from the ball joint. Nerves are still in trauma, which is probably why you can't feel much."

Karen's eyes filled with tears. "Will I ever... Will I... You know, ever walk again?"

Kind eyes regarded her as Faulkner gently lifted the left leg. "We have every hope. We'll know better after you've seen Dr. Cote. She's the best. For now, your job is to rest. I'll check in later today, okay?"

Karen nodded, lying back on the pillow, closing her eyes as the doctor slipped out.

When her brothers returned, they thought she was asleep, dried tears streaked down her round freckled cheeks. "Maybe we should let her rest?" Jonas whispered.

"Oh no, you don't," she said, eyes popping open. "Which one of you is going to tell me how this medical miracle took place? How did I get an appointment with Super Doctor so quickly?"

"Well, it's a bit circuitous, sis," Tim said, pulling up a chair beside her.

"It was Rich, wasn't it? Or his dad?"

Jonas nodded. "Muesse, the doc you saw last night, was Rich's college roommate. Then Muesse went to med school with Super Doc."

Karen closed her eyes. "I should have known."

Tim stroked her forehead. "You get some rest, sis. Mom and Dad'll be back soon."

She turned her head away to hide the tears. "I want to see him if he's still here."

The brothers locked eyes. "We'll see what we can do, baby," Jonas said. "Now get a good nap."

As she drifted off, Karen wondered if she was hallucinating. *Rich in the hospital? My savior, apparently. Why is he here? What do I say to him if he does pop in?*

"She was askin' for you, you know," Rex Miller said as they drove past Bayport on their way to Horseshoe Crab Cove. Shortly after breakfast, Rex had announced that he should get home to check in with Brick and get clothes for Faith, who refused to leave her daughter. Rich had volunteered to drive him. Although reluctant, Jonas had headed for the airport and Spark's plane that had been waiting several days to transport him westward. Tim had offered to stay with Faith until his father returned.

"Probably the meds she's on. Believe me, the last time your daughter was lucid, I was the last person she wanted to see."

"People change."

"She's got a long road ahead of her. Best to have it be as smooth as possible. No drama."

"Maybe, but it sure helps to have loved ones nearby."

"Rex, with all due respect, I'm not sure I fit that category."

"Then you're as dense as she is."

"You gonna need a ride back to Boston?" Rich asked.

"No, thanks. I'm taking Faith's car back so we'll be able to get home. Tim drove us, and he's gotta get back tonight. Karen's mom and I'll camp up there and let everyone else get on with their lives."

Both men lost in thought, neither spoke again until he turned the BMW down the long drive to Land's End. "Thanks, son," Rex said. "We owe you for bringin' in your friend and getting us an appointment with this Dr. Cote. Hope she's as good as they say she is."

"She is according to Jim, and I trust him. Karen's in good hands. Can I do anything for you or the farm? Errands in town or...?"

"I think we got it. What you can do for me is think about visiting our headstrong daughter."

"I'll take my cues from her."

"It's been my experience with our baby girl that she often says one thing and means another."

Rich smiled, turning to him. "Like when she's high on drugs and asks to see me?"

Rex laughed. "Touché, but in this case, I believe the wish to see the man she loves was genuine. Think about it."

Rich parked alongside the farmhouse. "Sure you're okay?" he asked as the older man hopped out.

"Right as rain. Thanks again. I expect we'll be seeing you soon."

CHAPTER 31

The next few days, Rich busied himself with work, resisting the urge to head back to Boston. He did check in with his sister Gail to hear updates from Tim, who was back and forth to the hospital every day. His own surgery and recovery had been almost forgotten in the aftermath of Karen's accident. Dr. Carina had still not okayed him to run. Instead, every afternoon, he took a break and went to the main house to use Richard's stationary bicycle, which was in the state-of-the-art gym in the farmhouse basement.

On a warm Thursday afternoon, his father found him cycling, engrossed in the latest *New Yorker*. "Hey, son, how's it going?"

Startled, Rich looked up. "Okay. How 'bout you?"

"Fine... Good... You've been working round the clock this week."

"Same schedule I always keep."

Richard sat on a bench beside him. "But you're meant to be recovering."

"I am, Dad. I feel great."

"Have you talked to Karen?"

One bushy eyebrow raised, Rich gave him a look. "No."

"Just asking. You know, the other one calls several times a day looking for you."

"Who, Sara?"

"Seems to be having a hard time tracking you down."

Sara... I really do have to do something about Sara. Since his return from Boston, he'd let all her calls go to voicemail. "Sorry. I didn't know that was happening. I'll take care of it."

"Anything you want to talk about?"

"No, thanks."

"Okay, just wanted to check. You know I'm always here for you, son. The last thing I want is for Morgan Enterprises to make you sick. I'm here. Your sisters are here. Any of us can take up the slack for a while so you can rest and visit your girl."

"Thanks, Dad. I'm fine, really." Clearly, his talk with Sara a week ago had not done the trick. Every message sounded more urgent. Despite her dramatic goodbye and exit from his house, she now seemed hell-bent on reconciliation. *I really have to talk to her.* Sighing, he grabbed his phone and punched in her number.

"Oh, thank goodness, sweetie!" she said. "I've been so worried."

"Hey, Sara. Could we meet for a drink later? Maybe the bar at Bannister's?"

"Love to. What time?"

"Can we say seven?"

"Perfect. How about dinner reservations?"

Might be iffy, he thought, *after what I have to say.* "Let's see how hungry we are. We can always eat at the bar."

"Great. See you then!"

As he walked back to the office, he considered what he should say. No matter what happened with Karen, he knew he had to end things with Sara once and for all.

"I WANT TO SEE HIM! WHY HASN'T HE COME?" KAREN ASKED, GAZING from parent to parent as they sat in Dr. Cote's light-filled waiting room.

Faith looked at her youngest child, pale, thin, and gaunt after not eating much for over a week. Slumped in a wheelchair, she seemed to have lost all her strength and vitality. "We think he's being respectful, baby. Trying to give you space to heal and be with your family."

"But I asked to see him. I told Jonas and Tim in the hospital. They promised to tell him."

The door to the inner office opened and a dark-skinned nurse with thick wavy hair and bright charcoal eyes stepped out. He was dressed in navy scrubs and orange Allbirds sneakers. "Ms. Miller, I'm Carlos? We're ready for you now."

Rex took hold of the wheelchair and wheeled her forward. "Here we go, Punky."

Dr. Cote's PA took all her information and sent them down to X-ray, a painful process which required her father and two techs to lift and position her. Karen bit her lip and remained stoic throughout, although Rex spied tears in her eyes as they gently placed her back in the wheelchair. Not for the first time, he wished he could go through this in her place.

After taking the elevator back up to the main floor, Carlos took control of the wheelchair and led them down the hall. A petite sandy-haired woman in a crisp white blouse, khakis, and sensible brown shoes stood at the doorway to one of the examining rooms. Her straight, shoulder-length hair was held back by glasses perched on her head, her only adornment the stethoscope around her neck. "Karen?" she asked as they neared the door.

"Yes."

"I'm Dr. Cote. Gretchen. Come on in."

After shaking hands with Faith and Rex, the physician turned her full attention to her patient. "How are you holding up?"

"Okay. My left leg's feeling better every day, and I've started to feel a little in my right one."

"Can you move your toes?"

Karen grimaced, but try as she might, her right foot lay limp and unresponsive. "What does it mean? I should be able to move by now, right?"

"Not necessarily. Your body has experienced major trauma. It's just beginning to heal." Gently, she began her examination. Karen's right leg was immobilized in a heavy black brace, the removal of which had caused considerable pain during the X-rays. Dr. Cote moved very slowly and carefully, pausing from time to time to take notes and re-examine the X-rays displayed on the opposite wall. Finally, she sat down on a stool, setting her clipboard aside.

"Many physicians would wait a while, but the kind of procedure I use has better outcomes if we operate early, then get the patient moving. I have an opening tomorrow. We would need to admit you to the hospital tonight, then do the pre-op and lab work for a nine a.m. surgery."

Karen's jaw dropped. "Tomorrow? I was thinking you'd say a month or so."

Dr. Cote smiled. "Normally, I book nine months to two years out, but I can never say no to Jim Muesse. He was very persuasive."

"Do you know his friend Rich Morgan? Jim's, I mean."

"Never met him, but Jim talked about him all the time when we were in med school. They were always going off on an adventure somewhere. Sounds like a great guy. Very generous and kind, according to Jim. Father's some kind of kazillionaire."

Karen smiled, suddenly feeling a bit woozy. "You've got that right."

"Punky, are you okay?" Rex asked, his blue eyes full of concern as he gazed at her.

"Of course she's not okay," Faith said, coming to stand next to Karen, gently smoothing hair from her forehead. "She's weak, tired, and in pain."

"Shall I step out and leave you three to decide about tomorrow?" Gretchen asked, her kind hazel eyes, moving between all three of them.

Karen shot her hand up. "No! I'm ready. Let's do it."

"Are you sure baby?" her mother asked, hand stroking her cheek.

"Yes."

Rex stepped forward, towering over the diminutive doctor. "Is it safe? What I mean to say is—if we waited till she gets her strength back, would that be the wiser course?"

"That's not an easy question. The operation is safe, as far as any surgery can be deemed safe. Waiting a month or two would definitely help her in regaining strength. I'm giving you my medical opinion related to her mobility. My medical opinion is that Karen will have the best chance of full restoration of the leg's functionality if we act now."

Faith gazed up at her. "You mean if we wait, she may not walk again?"

"I'm giving you my recommendation. That's the best I can do. I've assessed Karen's health and her legs, and I wouldn't recommend surgery now if I didn't think she could handle it."

Karen raised both hands. "Mom, Dad, I love you both, but this is my decision. I'm having the surgery tomorrow morning. Period. Now let's get me over to the hospital, pronto."

CHAPTER 32

"Hey, big brother," Gail Morgan said as he passed the front porch on his way to his car. Rich dreaded the evening and his meeting with Sara.

"Hey," he said, waving to Gail, Lucy, and Richard, who were sipping wine in the shade.

"Where's the fire?" Gail called. "Come have a drink."

Rich paused, smiling wearily. "Thanks, but I can't. Got to meet someone."

"Did Tim reach you?" his sister asked, stepping down from the porch, wineglass in hand.

"No, why?" He reached into his pocket to extract his cell phone, which had five missed calls. "Shit, I had it on mute for a conference call earlier. Why? What's happened?"

"Karen's having the hip replacement tomorrow."

Rich stared at her as if she'd grown horns and two heads. "What? I thought it was just today that she was seeing Gretchen Cote."

"It was, and Cote recommended operating immediately."

"Shit... Okay. I'll call Tim from the car. Gotta go. See ya."

"Want me to come with you?" his father called.

Rich waved over his shoulder. "Thanks, Dad, but I've got this."

As the three watched the BMW fly up the driveway in a cloud of dust, Gail turned to the others. "Geez, I hope by 'I got this,' he means he's going to go see her, tell her he loves her, and be done with it."

"He's got to break it off with the other one first," Richard said. The two women turned and stared over at him, and he shrugged. "Just sayin'."

BY THE TIME HE REACHED BANNISTER'S, RICH HAD REHEARSED HIS speech to Sara ten times. As he drove in, he spied her Honda parked near the bar entrance. Hopping out, he headed toward the door when he heard her call. He swiveled to find her standing beside the gate leading to the dock. She looked as if she was posing for a magazine shoot.

"Hey!" He waved as he approached her.

She wore a light peach sleeveless dress that flattered her slender frame, its vee neck revealing a hint of cleavage. Strappy sandals with five-inch heels accentuated her lithe, strong legs, and a soft shawl in swirling colors matched the dress. She looked beautiful, and she knew it.

"Pretty night, isn't it?"

"You look pretty too," he said, leaning down to peck her cheek.

She moved closed, arms circling his neck. "Is that any way to greet me after this long absence?"

Rich stepped back, taking hold of her arms and settling them at her side. "Let's go in, shall we?"

"Spoilsport," she said, endeavoring to keep her tone light and airy even as her brown eyes betrayed her disappointment and a hint of anger.

The bar was packed, but a couple had vacated a table with two stools near the window. Rich suggested they grab the table and gently propelled her forward. They both ordered white wine, and the waitress disappeared.

"So, how are you?" he asked.

"Okay. Been busy at the studio. The boss has been back and forth supporting her sister and niece. How's she doing, by the way?"

Rich shrugged. "All reports say okay."

She gave him a curious look. "I'm surprised you're free and not keeping vigil at her bedside wherever she is. I heard today she needs a hip replacement. That's pretty major."

Rich nodded as the waitress set down their drinks and a platter of cheeses, crackers, olives, and pickles, a Bannister's tradition when ordering cocktails. "Yes." He nodded to the waitress, who left them alone.

Sara reached across and took his hand. "So good to see you."

"Sara, I asked to meet because I want to be clear about my intentions and where I stand."

She squeezed his hand. "I hope you're going to say you're open to exploring us?"

He withdrew his hand from her grasp and put it in his lap. "No, I'm not. There's no easy way to say this, but I want to be clear. There is no us."

"Because she's pushed in between us."

"No... In fact, I've hardly seen or spoken to Karen since the Darn Yarners party. She was angry with me, rightfully so."

"Then what's going on? I'm here, and I love you."

"You're a wonderful person, but my heart is elsewhere, and that's where I want to be."

Her eyes blazed. "Even though she won't speak to you? This is craziness!"

"Maybe so, but you and I are over. I enjoyed our time together, but I'm going to spend my time, for as long as it takes, trying to make things work with Karen. I love her."

"You know she has a reputation for cut-and-run whenever a relationship gets serious?"

"I do."

"And you still want to take that chance when you have a sure thing here?"

"I'm sorry, Sara."

"Well, I am too!" She hopped off her stool and grabbed her clutch purse and shawl. "You have someone who loves you, cared for you after your surgery, and was ready to give her life for you! Instead, you're chasing a fly-by-night farm girl who wouldn't know love if she fell over it. You deserve each other. Goodbye, Rich!"

Sara turned and stomped out of the bar, slamming the door behind her.

That went well, he mused, heading to the bar to settle up. *Time to visit my fly-by-night farm girl.*

He said good night to the waitress. A huge grin on his face, he headed for his car.

"I'M FINE, MAMA!" KAREN SAID, WRESTING HER HAND FROM HER mother's grasp. "I want you and Dad to go home. They said they'd call when the surgery's over and it's time for you to get a good night's sleep."

"Baby, we don't want to leave you alone."

"I'm not a baby, and I'm fine. The nurses will take good care of me. Please take the night off. I'm begging you."

"Well... I'll chat with your dad when he comes back." Rex had stepped out to make a few phone calls and get them some sandwiches.

A nurse stepped into the spacious room with its Scandinavian-style furniture, the chairs and tables a soft blonde wood, the sleeper sofa's long lean lines reminiscent of a Nordic spa. Karen's hospital bed was much wider than the usual twin mattress and very comfortable. She was looking forward to a solitary, somewhat restful sleep. After a week of her parents' snoring, she'd had enough.

"How you doing?" Jody, the nurse, asked, coming to the bedside to check the monitor. The petite brunette managed to be efficient and nurturing, qualities which Karen appreciated.

Karen turned away. "Mom, why don't you go find Dad while I talk to Jody."

When the door closed behind Faith, Karen said, "Honestly, for your ears only, I'm scared to death about tomorrow, and I don't scare easily. Part of it is lack of sleep. Part is my family's constant hovering, but mostly, I'm scared that I'll never walk again."

"Dr. Cote's the best."

"That's what we keep hearing, but I still can't move or feel my right leg."

"Your left is progressing nicely, though, which is great because Dr. Cote's going to want you up and walking tomorrow evening."

"What!"

Jody smiled, patting her shoulder. "With support. PT will be in, and we'll assist with your walker."

"I don't have a walker."

"They'll deliver one tomorrow. I've got your meds, but I could ask for something to help you sleep. Would that be helpful?"

"Yes, please. The other thing that would be helpful is to ask my parents to go home. I love them, but I need some alone time."

"I'll see what I can do." Jody handed her a cup with several pills and a glass of water. After Karen swallowed them, she said, "I'll pop out and check about a sleep aid. Be back soon."

FAITH FOUND HER HUSBAND SITTING IN A SMALL WAITING AREA AT THE end of the hall, a brown bag from the cafeteria beside him. He grinned as she neared. Hey, sweetie. How's things?"

"She wants us to leave."

"I think that's a good thing."

"You do?" Faith plunked down beside him.

"Just heard from Rich. He called to see if he could drop in."

"And you told him yes?"

"Yup. Be good for her. Now let's you and I go say our good nights and take these sandwiches to go." He reached over and patted her knee.

CHAPTER 33

Rich parked in the side lot at Long Bridge Hospital and checked his phone. He half expected to find a voicemail warning him off, but there were no messages. As he looked around his car wondering what to bring with him, Karen's parents exited the hospital, holding hands. He hopped out and waved. "Hi, Millers!"

Both smiled and waved, waiting as he approached. *They both look like they've aged a decade in the last week,* he thought. *Sleep deprivation will do that.*

"Evening," he said, as Faith, then Rex hugged him.

"Oh, sweetheart, you're a sight for sore eyes. She'll be so pleased. She's been asking about you all week."

Rex patted his shoulder. "Thanks for coming, son."

Rich gave them both a look. "Are you sure about this?"

Faith winked. "You didn't hear it from us, but our baby's crazy about you. Never seen her this way about a man."

Rex took hold of her arm. "Come on, darling. Let the boy go in. Take good care of her, son."

"Have you eaten?" Faith asked.

"No, but I can—"

"Take these," she said, shoving the bag of sandwiches and snacks into his hands. "I have food at home for us. You'll need them more than we do."

"Thanks."

Rich stood still, watching until they reached their car before heading inside to the quietest hospital he'd ever been in with its carpeted hallways and soft lighting. He made his way to Karen's room, asking directions of several people along the way. When he arrived, he peeked in only to find her asleep, mouth open, tiny snores punctuating the silence. He walked to the bed, pulled up a chair, and sat, gazing at her. Even in her plain green hospital johnny, falling off her shoulder on one side, he thought she had never looked prettier. Gently, he drew the blanket over her thin bare shoulder.

"Hello my love," he whispered. "I'm here."

In answer, her eyes fluttered open, and she gave him a dreamy smile. "It's you... You came. I've been calling and calling for you."

"I know. I'm sorry." He took her hand. Careful not to disturb the IV, he drew it to his lips. "I'm here now...as long as you need me."

"You're here," she repeated, eyes blinking open and shut.

"Just gave her a pretty powerful sedative," a voice said from behind him. He turned toward the door. "I'm her nurse, Jody. I'll be here all night."

"I'm Rich. Ditto about the all-night part."

"That sofa pulls out into a bed. It's pretty comfortable, actually."

"I was going to sit with her."

"I promise she's not going to know you're here until morning. Might as well get some sleep."

When he glanced back at Karen, she was sleeping again. He gazed around the room and spied a small recliner near the window. After dragging it over, he replaced the chair by the bedside, leaving room for the nurse to get by.

"Good idea," Jody whispered as she stepped in to bring a fresh pitcher of water. "I'll bring you a blanket."

After the nurse departed, he gazed down at Karen. "I love you," he whispered, bending to kiss her softly. She murmured, then smiled, her eyes never opening. "Sleep, my darling girl, and I'll see you in the morning."

Leaning back in the recliner, he flung the blanket over himself, reached over, and took her hand and closed his eyes. *Not sure what tomorrow will bring, but I'm here now, baby.*

MIRACULOUSLY, HE SLEPT THROUGH THE NIGHT CURLED IN HIS RECLINER. When he opened his eyes, he found Karen lying on her side, gazing over at him. "Hey," she said softly.

He sat up. "Hey, yourself. What time is it?"

"A little after six. Jody just finished her shift. She says they'll be coming for me before long."

"That's good."

"Maybe."

"You okay?"

She shrugged, her hair all askew, eyes still sleepy. "I feel like I was hit with a baseball bat."

"That's probably the sedative they gave you."

"Mm... I had a really nice dream."

"Oh?"

"I dreamed you told me you loved me."

"Well, that was—"

"Good morning, Karen!" a booming voice said as a heavy-set redhead in sneakers and jungle-print scrubs strode in. "I'm Bertie. I'll be taking you down to pre-op. You ready?"

"Well, I... I wanted to—"

"Use the bathroom?"

"Something like that."

"I'll set up the bedpan." Bertie turned to Rich. "Hon, you may want step out? Give her some privacy?"

"Oh, of course," he said, hopping off the recliner.

Karen sat up, wincing. "Don't go far!"

"Be right outside."

A few minutes later, Bertie poked her head out. "Coast is clear."

Trying vainly to brush her snarly head of hair, Karen said, "I'd say I'm embarrassed, but after the past couple of weeks, I've learned not to care."

Rich smiled. "I hear you. Hospitalization and incapacity are humbling. But you don't need to be embarrassed. You look as beautiful as you ever have."

"Liar. Will you walk down with me?" she said, eyes pleading as she reached out her hand.

Rich took it, careful to stay out of the nurse's way. "Of course, if it's okay with Bertie."

Bertie gave him a thumbs-up. "Okay, folks, it's time." She pushed the call button behind Karen's bed, and within a minute, a young man in green scrubs appeared with a gurney, moving it alongside the bed. He then stepped around to the far side of the bed.

"Can I help?" Rich asked.

Bertie winked. "We've got it, hon. Okay, Les, on my count. One, two, three." The two of them lifted and slid Karen to the gurney. After Bertie tucked in blankets and checked Karen from head to toe, she said, "Let's blow this pop stand, shall we?"

"Will I be coming back here?" Karen asked.

"Sure will. That's the beauty of your somewhat unorthodox admittance. You're all unpacked and settled in."

As Bertie and Les wended their way down the hall, Rich walked alongside the gurney, holding Karen's hand.

"I'm so glad you're here," she said softly.

Rich smiled down at her. "Me too."

The next thirty minutes were a blur as doctors, nurses, and anesthesiologists prepped her for surgery. Rich sat quietly in the corner of the pre-op cubicle, unsure if he should stay or go. Finally, a new nurse, Gina, stepped in. "Hey, Karen, how're you doing?"

"Okay," she replied, her voice faint and hoarse.

"I'm going to put something in your IV to make you sleepy, then we'll be heading down to have the spinal, okay?"

Karen nodded.

After Gina departed, he rose and came beside her, tucking errant strands of hair under her surgical cap.

"Glamourous look, huh?"

"You look beautiful." He leaned over and kissed her forehead. "I'm thinking this might be my cue to take off?"

"Can you wait till they come for me?" she asked as her eyes closed.

"Of course," he said softly.

Five minutes later, Gina appeared. "It's time."

"I think she's asleep," Rich whispered.

"Good girl," Gina said, cranking down the gurney and releasing the brakes.

Rich bent down, whispered, "I love you," and kissed her softly. Karen smiled, but her eyes stayed shut.

He followed them to the elevator. As the doors closed, Gina said, "Don't worry. We'll take good care of her."

CHAPTER 34

"Stop it!" Karen screamed. She shoved the walker aside and flopped onto the sofa. "I can't do this anymore!" It was three weeks since her surgery, and she still had no use of her right leg despite hours of daily physical therapy.

Janice Penny, the visiting physical therapist, watched her fall, calmly standing nearby. Rich had just arrived and was sitting ten feet away by the window. The Millers had converted their light-filled sunporch into Karen's bedroom so she wouldn't have to tackle stairs. The long narrow space was filled with plants, and an eclectic assortment of comfortable furniture lined its walls—two sofas, matching armchairs with faded canvas covers, a few side tables and Karen's bed against the inside wall.

"Can I help?" he asked, trying to keep his voice soft and reassuring.

"No, thanks. You shouldn't even be here watching this pathetic charade. Who are we kidding? My leg is useless, and it's always going to be."

"But Dr. Cote said it takes time," he said.

"Dr. Cote doesn't know shit, and neither does anyone else. I know what this feels like—nothing!"

"Maybe we'll give the walking a break today and concentrate on stretching and moving?" Janice said, smiling as she stepped toward the sofa. She reached out both arms. "Shall we begin?"

"No! I want to be by myself!"

Faith Miller stepped onto the porch. "Hey, baby, what's going on? Janice is here to help you."

Karen's arm shot up. "Not you too, Mama! I just need time by myself. Everyone's been hovering for three weeks. I'm going crazy!"

Rich watched, saying little. Karen looked as though she'd lost thirty pounds. Her hair was tied back in a sloppy ponytail, curly tendrils falling over her face, and she was dressed in shorts and a T-shirt. Her feet were bare despite Janice's earlier attempts to have her put on sneakers. Her left leg had almost returned to normal, but the right was still encased in a brace from waist to knee. As yet, she couldn't put weight on it. All her standing movements were accomplished by her upper body and left leg.

"You know what," Janice said. "I think Karen's right. We should take the day off. I'll be back Friday, and I'll leave today's exercises for you to help her perform, three times daily if possible."

Karen scowled at her. "Like that's gonna happen."

Faith smiled at the physical therapist. "Perhaps you're right, dear. Come on, I'll show you out. You can do your paperwork at the kitchen table." The two disappeared, closing the French doors behind them.

Rich came to sit beside her. Karen had slowly maneuvered herself to a sitting position and was now resting her left leg on a stool, the right straight out in front of her. "You okay?"

"No. I'm sick of this."

"Of course you are."

He tried to place his arm around her, but she shrugged it off. "You don't understand. Nobody does. I'm surrounded by Pollyannas. This is my life, and it really sucks. Everyone's got to accept it and get used to it."

"I get it. It totally sucks, but it's only been three weeks and only two since the surgery."

"Two weeks, two months, two years. None of that makes a

difference when I've made zero progress. Nothing, nada!"

"What does Dr. Cote say?"

"Same bullshit. Give it time, but I don't believe her."

He reached over, intending to take her hand, then thought better of it. "When do you see her next?"

"Friday morning."

"Maybe she'll have some insight?"

Karen shrugged, leaning back and closing her eyes.

"Can I get you something?"

"Iced tea?" she replied, eyes still closed.

When he returned, she was sitting up straighter and appeared to have made an attempt to brush her hair. She gave him a weary smile as he handed her the tea, then patted the sofa beside her.

"I sure love to see that smile," he said as he sat.

"I'm sorry for my earlier behavior. After all you've done the past two weeks, that's the last thing you needed to see."

"Apology unnecessary, and there's no place I'd rather be."

"But you shouldn't be."

"Excuse me?"

"You shouldn't be here."

"Of course, if it's easier for you to have PT in private, I understand."

"No, it's not that. When I see Gretchen Cote, I'm going to readjust that schedule anyway. No, what I mean is that I don't want you to come back."

Rich's chest constricted, and he stared at her. "What?"

She turned to face him. "I love you, Rich, I really do. I hope you know that, but this relationship has run its course. You know my reputation. This is what I do—love 'em and leave 'em."

"But we've barely begun."

"Some last longer than others."

"This is your injury talking."

"Not entirely. I mean yes, I'm in a shitty place right now, most likely forever, but I'd have been breaking this off soon anyway."

"I don't believe you."

"I'm sorry, I really am, but I'm not changing my mind. Thanks for everything and for being so loving and kind, but I'd like you to leave now."

"Okay, you need some alone time. I get it. I'll be back tomorrow."

"No, you won't," she said, eyes downcast. "I won't see you, so please do not come back."

"But Karen." He reached out to embrace her, but she pushed him away.

"Rich, I'm serious! Now go."

Rich stood. "Okay, then. Hope you feel better," he said, then walked out of the room. As he passed the kitchen, Faith called to him.

"She's our firecracker, honey. Can't take it personally."

"She's asked me not to come back," he said, unsuccessful in keeping tears from his eyes.

"She doesn't mean it."

"I think she does."

"Well, I'll have a talk with her."

"Please don't. She's got so much healing to do. The least we can do is let her call the shots."

Faith stood up and came around the table to hug him. "You're a wonderful man, Rich Morgan, and this family owes you so much. I don't know where we'd be if you hadn't been here."

Rich returned the embrace. "Thanks, but I wouldn't have been anywhere else. You'll let me know if you need anything or if she changes her mind about seeing me?"

"In a heartbeat. Do you want to stay for dinner?"

"Thanks, but I'm eating at the farm."

As Rich drove down the Land's End driveway, he felt as if a vital organ had been ripped from his body. His lifeblood, his core -- gone. *How will I live without seeing her? Her sweet smile, lapis-blue eyes, soft dewy skin that, until the past few weeks, always smelled of honeysuckle and the ocean.* As he drove through town, he thought about the intensity of the past few weeks. He was so far behind at work, he doubted he'd ever catch up. *Well, at least I have plenty of time to try,* he mused. *Plenty of time to heal a shattered heart too.*

CHAPTER 35

"Happy now?" Faith asked as she set a glass of lemonade beside her daughter.

Karen stared straight ahead. "Don't start, Mother!"

"Just answer me this—why did you push him away? He loves you and wants to help."

"Well, he can't, because I'm a cripple, and I will not saddle him with this." She waved a hand down her right leg as she struggled to sit up.

Looks like a bird caught in a hurricane, her mother mused. *All her feathers ruffled and askew.* "You don't know that. Dr. Cote says—"

"Screw Dr. Cote! I'm sick to death hearing about Dr. Cote. She doesn't know shit. Why'd I even bother with the surgery when it did nothing. Nothing!"

"You don't know that."

"But I do! Now please leave me alone. I mean it, Mother. And no more mention of Rich. If you or Dad let him into this house, I will never speak to you again."

Might not be such a bad thing, Faith thought, gazing at her daughter with sad eyes. "Okay, sweetie. Call if you need anything." She stepped out and gently closed the French doors behind her.

"Not having a good day, is she?" Rex said as Faith came back to the kitchen. After a day in the fields, her husband was covered from head to toe with grit and mud.

"No, she is not, and don't you dare sit down with those filthy overalls. Undress in the laundry room and get up to the shower."

"I thought I'd pop my head in."

Faith crossed the room and kissed his grimy cheek. "Shower first. Let her cool down. She's just sent Rich away and told him not to come back."

"Aw, that's not good."

"We're forbidden to let him through the door."

Rex shook his head. "Well, that's not happening."

"Yes, it is. It's what she wants, and we have to go along for now, anyway. Now git!"

RICHARD MORGAN STARED DOWN THE LONG TABLE AT HIS ELDEST. IN addition to himself and Lucy, they'd been joined for dinner by Weezie, Gail, Tim, and Pam, as well as Lucy's sister Harriet, and Kyle. "Hey, son, you're looking pretty glum. Everything okay?"

Rich gave him a look, regretting his decision to come to supper instead of going home to lick his wounds. "Not really."

"Anything we can do to help?" his father asked as Lucy nudged him and Gail shook her head.

Rich smiled at his sister. "It's okay. You may as well know, all of you. Karen's kicked me out and asked me not to come back."

"Uh-oh... Miss Love-'Em-and-Leave-'Em strikes again," Weezie said, waving a slice of cornbread just plucked from a basket on the table.

Gail gave her sister a sharp look. "What a silly thing to say!" She turned to her brother. "This is her pain talking. She'll change her tune once she starts to heal."

Rich shrugged. "I don't think so. Not this time."

"I'm so sorry to hear this," Harriet said. "Karen's my oldest friend, but she's being a horse's ass. Excuse my language."

"Horse's ass or not, it's over," he said.

Lucy gazed from her husband to his oldest. "She cares for you. Very much. I'm sure she does."

Rich gave her a wan smile. "Can we change the subject, please?"

"Why not," Richard said. "What's new down at the stables? Your Kiki's working out very well, Kyle. Can't thank you enough for bringing her to us."

Weezie rolled her eyes. "Spends way too much time hanging around Coop. Why does she think she has to oversee the shoeing?"

Both competitors for the attentions of the handsome blacksmith, Weezie and Kiki had gotten off to a rocky start. This was no secret to anyone at the table.

Tim grinned. "I'm sure Coop doesn't mind."

Kyle nodded, mischief in his eyes. "She's probably trying to spend as much time as she can getting to know the horses. Especially important with the wild ones."

Weezie frowned. "Humph, more like getting to know the blacksmith!"

As Callie began to clear the dishes, Lucy decided a change of subject was in order. She turned to Pam. "How are the wedding plans coming?"

The group spent the rest of dinner discussing Pam and Sandy's upcoming nuptials. Rich slipped out after dessert, his father on his heels. As they reached his car, Richard put a hand on his shoulder. "She'll come around, son. Her healing's barely begun."

"Maybe, Dad. For now, I'm going to give her the space she wants and stay away."

"You know best. See you in the morning. Vineyard at nine?"

"I'll be there. Thanks for dinner."

"You want to move back home for a few weeks?"

Rich grinned. His father's answer to all problems was to move back home. "I'm good, Dad. Night."

CHAPTER 36

"You gotta move on, brother," Ben Morgan said as he and Teddy stood chatting with Rich at Sandy's. The occasion was Sandy's bachelor party. The club was open, crowded with patrons listening to a popular local band. They'd closed the porch for the bachelor party, which included Sandy's dad. Cesar had taken a rare night off from the restaurant and now sat at a table with Richard Morgan and his brother Ben.

Rich's eyebrows went up as he gave his brother a look. "And how would you propose I do that?"

"I'm sure there are plenty of women around," Teddy said. "You could probably pop inside and grab one right now."

"Ha-ha. When have you known me to be the grab-a-woman type."

Teddy chuckled. "What happened to the lovely yoga instructor?"

"History," Rich said, gazing over at his father and friends. "Can we talk about anything else but my pathetic, nonexistent love life?" He gestured toward their dad. "Look at those guys—they managed to do it right."

"The silver foxes," Ben said. "Don't worry. We'll get there someday. And don't forget, Dad had a two-decade dry spell until Lucy."

The three brothers strolled over to join the groom-to-be, who stood talking to his brothers Vincent, Michael, and Raffi, and the Miller brothers. Murph, Sandy's assistant manager, and a few of the club employees drifted in and out, taking turns running things inside and popping in on their boss's party. Kyle Morgan had also come to be with his father, who had just flown in that morning.

"THIS IS PERFECT," PAM SIGHED, LEANING BACK ON THE TEAK BENCH IN the evening twilight. They were in Laura's Garden. At first, she had refused her sisters' offer to host a bachelorette party, but had finally agreed to have wine and appetizers in the garden before heading to Bluewater Seafood for dinner. Aided by Leonora and Lucy, Weezie had organized several silly games involving trivia and charades, but they were now over, and everyone was relaxing with wine and simple appetizers prepared by Callie.

"I wonder what the guys are doing?" Gail asked.

Pam shook her head. "Hopefully nothing crazy. Sandy promised. Besides, it's at the club, so he can't go too nuts."

"Are you happy?"

Pam smiled. "Blissfully."

"May I join you?" Harriet Morgan strolled up, wine in hand. She wore a sleeveless floral print dress, its vee neckline surprisingly low. Below the fitted waist, the skirt flared to just below her knees. She wore strappy sandals and silver jewelry, her chestnut hair falling around her slender shoulders.

"Of course," Pam said. "I love that dress. Did you get it locally?"

"Catalog," Harriet said as she took a seat beside them. "Emory's. It's a small dress shop in Jacksonville, Florida. A friend at school told me about it. I've been trying to jazz up my wardrobe. Move away from the pioneer woman look."

"Well, you succeeded in that little number," Pam said.

Harriet blushed crimson. "You know your fiancé is the most gorgeous man in the village."

Pam smiled. "Your husband's no slouch, and neither is hers," she added, pointing to Gail.

Gail nodded. "We sure are surrounded by a lot of gorgeous men. I was sorry Karen decided not to come."

Harriet set down her wine, gazing around the garden. "I know... I was hoping her mom could persuade her. I was hoping they'd both come."

"Faith would have been more bummed if Rosa was here, or Helen." Sandy's mother, Rosa, was at the Grille holding down the fort so her husband could attend the bachelor party.

"Our mom's not much for parties," Melania Rodriguez said, passing by.

"Your sister's not here either," Gail said. "I was looking forward to meeting her."

"She flies in tomorrow. Can't stay long, never does," Melania said, pausing. "Sorry, didn't mean to eavesdrop."

"No worries. Join us, please," Pam said, indicating a nearby chair.

Faith Miller popped her head around the sunporch door. As usual, Karen was stretched out, book in hand, half asleep. "They'll be leaving for Bluewater soon, sweetie. Are you sure you wouldn't like to meet them for supper?"

"Very sure, thanks, Mom."

"I'll bring our supper out here, then."

Karen shook her head. "Not for me. I'm not hungry."

"Baby, you've got to eat. You're getting thin as a rail."

"I'll grab something later."

Good luck with that, Faith thought, leaving her. "Holler if you want anything."

As soon as her mother vanished, unbidden tears sprang up, and Karen reached for the tissue box. She wasn't even sure why she was crying. *Is it missing Rich, or the bleak prospect of the rest of my life? Will I ever emerge from the darkness?*

CHAPTER 37

"He's a really good guy," Jonas Miller said as he and Karen drove out of town on her way to Dr. Cote's. She had insisted her brother drive her to escape her mother's hovering. Jonas had returned from Arizona for the wedding. His brother Rex was also in town for a few days. Sandy Rodriguez had gone through school with their brother, Brick, but the three of them had been thick as thieves throughout their childhood.

"Not you too," she sighed, leaning back in the seat, closing her eyes. "Why do you think I refused to let Mom drive me?"

"She's doing her best, sis."

"I know, I know... I love our parents more than life itself. It's just... This sucks." She tapped the top of her leg brace. "And I'm still adjusting to life as a paraplegic."

"You don't know that."

"Oh yes, I do. I have no feeling in this leg. Nada."

"What's the doc been saying?"

"What she always says. Give it time. I have zero interest in seeing her today to hear the same drivel."

"You're comin' tonight, right?" he asked, referring to the rehearsal dinner hosted by Sandy's parents at their popular town restaurant.

"Haven't decided. I love the Grille's food. My favorite...so maybe."

Despite Pam and Sandy's efforts to keep it small, between the Miller, Rodriguez, and Morgan families, the dinner had grown to over seventy people. Pam's aunt and uncle, Ben and Leonora Morgan, were coming from Arizona as well as town friends and all the Darn Yarners. With the guest list for the wedding now topping hundred and fifty, the bride and groom had thrown up their hands and given Richard Morgan permission to do whatever he wanted at the farm, where the ceremony and reception would be held.

As they pulled into the medical center parking lot, Jonas peered over at his sister to find her rosy cheeks streaked with tears. "Hey, sis, it's gonna get better. I promise."

"I love him," she sobbed, covering her face.

"Course you do. That's gonna work out too."

"No, it is not. I refuse to stick him with this."

Jonas reached over an took her hand. "Don't you think that's his choice?"

"No." She yanked her hand away and turned to the car door. "Let's go in and get this over with."

A WAVE OF SADNESS WASHED OVER RICH AS HE WATCHED HIS SISTER Pam standing beside her fiancé. The couple stood in the barn door listening to pastor Anna Goodspeed's instructions. Sandy's arm was draped over her shoulder, and Pam leaned into him, head on his chest. *Will I ever find that kind of love?*

Surrounding the couple were most of the wedding party, Gail, Pam's maid of honor, and her bridesmaids Weezie and Ava and Elise Nolan. Murph O'Neill was Sandy's best man. His brothers Michael, Vincent, and Raffi, were his groomsmen. Rosa and Cesar, at the restaurant prepping for dinner, had not come out to view the rehearsal.

Richard came to stand next to his oldest. "Your time will come, son." His father could always read him like a book.

Rich shrugged. "Maybe. For now, it's enough to be happy for

them. Wish we could bottle up the kind of love they have. Look at them."

Richard nodded. "They'll have their ups and downs, but if I was a betting man, I'd bet on their happiness. After all, she's a therapist, and he runs the most successful bar on the East Coast."

Rich smiled, raising one eyebrow. "If that's your recipe for success, heaven help the rest of us!"

"Hey, guys," Lucy said, coming to put her arm around her husband.

Richard turned and kissed the top of her head. "Hi, beautiful. I thought you were having lunch with your mom and sister?"

"Mom's off with Leonora, and Harriet went out to Land's End to see Karen."

Her stepson's face fell at the mention of Land's End. "You okay?" she added.

"Fine, no worries," Rich answered, not entirely successful in his attempt to sound fine.

Lucy gazed over at the bride and groom. "Wasn't it smart of Anna to hold the rehearsal midday rather than dragging everyone over just before tonight's dinner?"

The thirty-something pastor wore jeans and a flowery peasant blouse, her curly reddish-brown hair tied back under a frayed straw hat. Barefoot, she'd discarded her Birkenstock sandals the moment she stepped into the backyard.

Richard nodded. "She's a wise woman indeed. Such an asset to the village."

"We only hope we can keep her," Lucy said. "Excuse me, guys." Giving her husband a hug and patting Rich's shoulder, she headed toward the trio to ask if they wanted something to drink.

"You're a lucky man, Dad," he said as they watched her go.

"Don't I know it. And you're gonna get there too. What say we head down to the stables and see what's goin' on? Leave these guys to rehearse."

As she alit from her car, Harriet spied Faith and Rex Miller on the farmhouse porch, cold drinks in hand. "Hi, sweetie!" Faith called, waving.

Harriet waved back. "Afternoon. How are you both?"

"Playin' hooky," Rex called. "Should be on the tractor. What can I get you?"

Harriet raised her arm, indicating the water bottle she held. "Nothing, thanks, I'm good. Thought I'd stop by and visit with Karen."

"How kind you are, dear," Faith said. "We are not in the best of moods. She and Jonas just returned from the surgeon's office."

"Oh dear, bad news?"

Faith shook her head. "No news, really. Dr. Cote is optimistic, but the truth is, she doesn't know. No one knows whether the leg will ever be right."

Harriet paused, leaning against the porch railing. "It's so soon, though, isn't it?"

"That's what we keep telling her, but you know your friend. She's never happy unless she's going a hundred miles a minute."

"You're right about that."

"Doesn't help that she broke up with her nice fella," Rex whispered as he peered over his shoulder.

"Well, I'll do my best to cheer her up. If you think she's not too tired for visitors?"

Faith waved her hands. "You? Never. Now, go right in, and don't be offended if she bites your head off."

Harriet knocked on the sunporch door. "Hey," she said softly. "Okay if I come in?"

She was answered with a grunt, which she took as a yes, and pushed open the door.

"Not much fun in here," Karen said, struggling to sit up.

"Can I get you anything?"

"A new leg would be great, or maybe a shotgun so I can blow my brains out."

Harriet pulled a chair up in front of the sofa, patting Karen's left knee. "Hey, it's not that bad, is it?"

"It's not good, that's all I know."

"What'd the doc say?"

"Nothing. Absolutely nothing. She doesn't know shit. No one does. And meanwhile, I might as well have had my right leg amputated. Lot of good it does me as a dead weight."

"I'm so sorry," Harriet said.

"Me too. Maybe it's punishment for all my wicked ways."

"You haven't had a wicked way in your life!"

"All the guys I've left at the altar? All the grief I've given my parents over the years?"

Harriet observed her friend, who appeared to have lost thirty pounds. Her T-shirt and shorts hung on her, her arms and legs spindly and pale, her face gaunt.

"Stop beating yourself up."

"I can't."

"It's going to get better, sweetie."

"How? I'm a cripple, and I've pushed away the person I love most in the world."

"Well...your body needs time to heal. It hasn't been long at all for this kind of injury."

"When did you become Doctor Know-It-All?"

Harriet eyed her friend. "And as for the man, he's not going anywhere. You can patch that up when you're feeling stronger."

"Never. I will never stick him with this. Never, never, never. Better to rip the bandage off now and be done with it."

"That's the most ridiculous thing I've ever heard."

Karen ran her fingers through her curly hair. "I wish everyone would leave me alone to make the decisions that are right for me."

"What about Rich? What about what's right for him?"

"Harriet Morgan... Geez I still can't get used to the name change. Anyway, you know I love you like a sister. More than my sister, if truth be told. I need for you to support me on this." She reached out a thin arm. "I don't think I can do this without you."

Harriet took her hand. "Of course. I'm here for you. Promise."

Karen lay back and took a deep breath, tears rimming her eyes. "Thank you."

"You're coming tonight, right?"

"As I told my brother, I'm coming for the food. I love the Grille."

"I'm glad."

"Jonas has promised me that if I start to freak out, I can give him the signal, and he'll whisk me out."

"Well, if you can't get his attention, Kyle and I can do the same. I'll keep my eye on you. Sound good?"

"Thanks," Karen said, her eyes fluttering open and closed. "You know, I think I might take a short nap."

"Good idea. I'll see you tonight." Harriet bent over and hugged her.

When the sunporch doors closed, the tears flowed. *Not sure how I'll deal with seeing him so soon, but at least I've got my escape plan,* Karen thought.

CHAPTER 38

Shortly after seven the Morgan family descended on The Grille. "How'd the rehearsal go?" Rosa Rodriguez asked her soon-to-be daughter-in-law.

Pam gave her a thumbs-up as Rosa hugged Lucy, whispering, "Is Mother coming?"

"Yes, Harriet's bringing her and Hazel." Hazel was Lucy's youngest sister who lived in Boston and worked for an international tours company.

"What about your other sisters?" The older woman's violet eyes sparkled with warmth. At sixty-nine, she was the oldest of the Darn Yarners, but you'd never know it. Her thick, dark hair hadn't a hint of gray, and her round face was unwrinkled even after six children and a lifetime of hard work. Short, plump, and strong as an ox, Rosa moved with grace and agility as she greeted her guests.

"Clara and Will should be here any minute. They're staying at the farmhouse," she added, referring to her third sister and her husband.

"Did Clara's kids come? It's been ages since we've seen them."

Lucy leaned close and whispered, "They weren't invited. With all our huge families, they were trying to keep the guest list down."

"Well, next summer, the Darn Yarners will organize a reunion and include *everyone!* Excuse me, dear." With that, Rosa rushed off toward her husband, who stood with Sandy and his brothers.

"She's a whirling dervish, isn't she?" Rich said.

Lucy nodded. "She certainly is. How're you holding up? Your dad's worried about you."

"You know me. Unflappable Rich."

"Flappable or not, you've been through a lot this summer. We forget to even ask how you're recovering from your surgery."

"Not ready to run a marathon, but I feel okay. I've been doing some light jogging."

"You've run quite a few marathons, haven't you?"

He nodded. "Mostly local, wherever we've lived. I'd like to run New York and maybe the Marine Corps Marathon in DC someday."

"That's one of my favorites. Rob, my former husband, and I ran it before we had kids."

"You still run some, don't you?"

"Not like that. I got pneumonia ten years ago, and whatever happened to my lungs, it's hard for me to run in the winter months."

"Bummer."

"Think you'll get back to long-distance running?" she asked.

"Maybe. Karen and I were planning to run the New Bedford Half Marathon."

She squeezed his arm. "Someday. Don't give up hope."

"Are we talking about running or romance?"

Lucy smiled. "Both!" As she looked toward the front door, her expression changed. "Oh look, here come the Millers. My, she's lost weight, hasn't she?"

Rich watched as Jonas pushed Karen's wheelchair forward. "Sure has. Can I get you something to drink?"

"That would be lovely, thanks. I wonder where your father's gotten to?"

As Rich headed for the bar, his expression grave, Pam caught him. "This is my wedding, big brother. I want everyone to be happy, including you."

He paused to hug her. "I am happy. Delirious, in fact."

"Liar."

He kissed her forehead. "I'm happy for you, sis. That's enough for me. I'm getting Lucy a drink. You want one?"

"Not that way!" Karen whispered, turning to poke her brother's arm.

"Ow! What was that for?"

"I'd rather not run into Rich. Take me that way. Harriet and Kyle are over there." As she spoke, Karen felt a lump in her throat. Her voice betrayed her feelings as she held back tears. He looked so handsome dressed casually in a blue sport shirt and khakis. As he waited by the bar, she watched his now-familiar gestures as he brushed hair from his forehead in conversation with another guest. *You can do this*, she told herself as they made their way across the crowded room.

Dinner was a lively affair with waitstaff serving course after course from the menu Cesar had created especially for the evening. Platters of antipasto and a variety of appetizers began the feast, followed by a saffron-infused cioppino loaded with fish, scallops, lobster, and clams. Diners had many choices for their main course—beef, pork, chicken, eggplant parmesan, white and red lasagna, three kinds of ravioli, each with its own sauce, and a number of other pasta dishes.

"And I thought we put on a feed at the ranch," Ben Morgan Senior said, a forkful of pasta in hand. "What will they do with the leftovers?"

"They go to a local soup kitchen," Lucy said. "The Rodriguez family are incredibly generous that way, all of them. Sandy supports a number of local charities almost single-handedly and his parents donate a ton of food each week. Raffi's law firm does a lot of pro bono work in Bayport."

Rich nodded. "Service is in their DNA."

"But you'd never know it," Richard said. "In fact, they wouldn't like us broadcasting any of this, especially the groom. Sandy's very private about his philanthropy."

"As are you, brother dear," Leonora said, smiling across the table at her brother-in-law.

"You're no slouches either," Richard said. "Aren't we lucky we've done so well and can share it with others." As he spoke, he gazed over at his eldest. Rich's green eyes reflected sadness. His father followed his son's gaze—Karen Miller. Sandwiched between her brothers Rex and Jonas, she looked impossibly thin and pale, her blouse appearing to be three sizes too big.

He caught Rich's eye and winked before turning to his brother. "So you lucky ducks are about to have Jonas Miller as a neighbor, right?"

Ben chuckled. "That's Spark's doing, but what a great kid."

Leonora rolled her eyes. "Man, darlin'. Spark's new engineer hasn't been a kid for a long time."

"Well, we've sure enjoyed getting to know that nice young man. He's based in Tucson, but has been up to the Valley several times. Knows his way around horses too. Even offered to help my son and Harley with the pack trips."

"He did grow up on a farm," Lucy said. She took a bite of asparagus lasagna and groaned. "Oh my goodness! Cesar makes the best pasta in the world."

After dinner, Rich excused himself and headed toward his brothers Ben and Teddy, who were chatting with Lucy's sister Clara and her husband. Before he reached the group, he glanced to the side and spied Karen alone at the table, her family nowhere in sight.

Swallowing hard, he changed direction. "Hey," he said when he stood next to her.

She looked like a baby bird, her arms lost in the sleeves of her blouse, cheeks hollow and pale. So unlike the robust rosy-cheeked farmer she'd been a month ago.

"Hey," she said softly.

"How're you doing?"

She shrugged. "'Bout the same."

"Wasn't your appointment with Dr. Cote today?"

"Yup." She stared straight ahead, refusing to meet his eyes.

"Sorry, I didn't mean to pry," he said. "Would you rather I leave you alone?"

"I'm not a whole lot of fun to be around right now."

"I miss you," he said softly. "I hope as time goes on, we can at least be friends."

She shrugged. "Maybe." Her eyes filled up, and she looked away.

"Oh, geez, Karen. I'm sorry. Last thing I want to do is upset you." Rich reached out his hand, then pulled back.

She straightened up, lips set. "Can you do me a favor?"

"Anything."

"Can you get one of my brothers? I need to go home."

"I can take you. I have my car."

"No, thanks. I see Jonas at the bar. Please tell him I need to go *now*."

Reluctant to leave her, he leaned down. "I'll see you tomorrow, then?"

"Maybe. I'm not sure I'm coming. Please, Rich, I need to go home."

Rich's chest ached as he watched Jonas push the wheelchair to the door, his father and mother on either side.

Night, sweet girl, he thought. *Will you ever come back to me?*

CHAPTER 39

Wedding day upon them, the farmhouse and yard bustled with activity. "You look beautiful my darling," Richard said. He held out his arm to Pam. "Your mother would have been so pleased and proud."

Rich came upstairs to tell the two the bridal party was ready and smiled at his sister.

Pam looked ethereal in a pale pink off-the-shoulder gown that fell to midcalf. Her strawberry-blonde hair was swept up in a chignon, her mother's pearls and matching earrings her only jewelry save the glittering three-carat diamond ring on her left hand.

"Dad's right, you look amazing. Rodriguez is a lucky man. I hope he knows it."

Pale blue eyes gazed at him, tears glistening. "Thanks, big brother. You look pretty darn handsome yourself."

Rich chuckled. "It's the suit." All the groomsmen and the fathers of the bride and groom were in Armani summer-weight tuxedos.

"No, it isn't. You are a gorgeous man inside and out. I just hope Karen Miller comes to her senses."

"This is your day, Pammy. Don't fret about me."

She laughed, taking her father's arm. "You haven't called me

Pammy since I was ten. And I will fret, because this is my day and I want everyone to be happy. Come on, Dad, let's do this."

Richard winked at his son. "Hear, hear! Lead the way, son. Time to get a move on."

Anna Goodspeed stood under a flower-bedecked arbor at the top of the rise, Laura's bench beside her. The fields stretched out to the north and the river lay eastward. They had mowed a swath of field around the bench and chairs formed concentric circles around the arbor. Rich followed his sisters and the Rodriguez brothers, Elise Nolan on his arm. His sister Gail came next, then a cluster of flower girls, including Sandy's daughter Maisie, Ava's daughters Sasha and Laura, and Gus and Lynn's daughters Dulcie and Sorcha. The older girls held the little ones' hands and Ava's son Cameron came last, holding a small wooden box with the rings. Finally, as Richard and Pam climbed the hill, the string quartet began playing "Here Comes the Sun."

Karen sat with her brothers, her sister-in-law, Susie, Brick's wife beside her. Susie leaned toward her, whispering. "Have you ever seen so many gorgeous men in one place?"

"Shush!" Karen hissed, but Susie was right. Sandy Rodriguez was movie-star handsome, as were his brothers; however, she only had eyes for the tall, slender eldest Morgan brother who stood alongside with his brothers Teddy and Ben. While not groomsmen, Pam had insisted they stand up with them. For a second, his eyes scanned the crowd, searching for her. When their eyes met, his gaze softened and he smiled before turning to his beautiful sister and her groom.

THE RECEPTION WAS CASUAL, BUFFET TABLES SET UP AROUND THE BARN'S interior. Small tapas-size plates were set out, and waitstaff continually replenished them as guests sampled cool delicious littlenecks from the raw bar, stuffed quahogs, small skewers of swordfish, shrimp, and scallops, roasted vegetables, and plentiful summer salads, breads and appetizers.

"Can I get you a plate Punky?" Rex Miller said, approaching his youngest who sat in the shade.

Karen shrugged. "Thanks, Dad. I'm not very hungry, but you know what I like, so I'd take a little. And I'd love a glass of red wine."

It was on his lips to ask if she should have alcohol, but he simply nodded. "Be right back."

She demanded that they leave her wheelchair in the car, so her brothers had carried her up the hill to the ceremony, then back down. Once they parked her in a comfortable chair, she insisted they go and have fun. Susie and Brick were nearby, chatting with townspeople but keeping an eye on her. Karen felt pathetic and small and a nuisance to them all.

Rich and Elise Nolan stood near the barn entrance, surveying the crowd. "Your girl's having a rough time, isn't she?" she said.

"Not my girl."

"Oh, I'm sorry, I thought...well Pam told me—"

"We were dating, but not anymore." He wanted to say more, but didn't know his sister's colleague well.

"I was so sad to hear about her accident. Devastating."

He nodded, his expression serious. "Yes, it was."

"I apologize," she said. "I didn't mean to pry. Occupational habit. Please forgive me."

Rich smiled. "No worries. Tell me, how are you and Pam enjoying your new digs? What a great spot, right across from the garden."

SANDY'S BEST MAN, MURPH O'NEILL, STARTED THE TOASTS WITH A somewhat raucous retrospective of his boss's "luck with the ladies." Rich looked over to find Pam as white as a sheet. As he wondered if he should interrupt the well-meaning Murphy, Lucy whispered, "Oh dear." Her eyes were on her best friend and business partner, Lolly LaSalle, the groom's ex-wife, who did not seem to be upset.

"Think I should interrupt?" Rich whispered.

Lucy shrugged. "Lolly appears to be unfazed, thank goodness. Let's hope she's finally put her marriage behind her."

As Rich sat wondering when Murph would sit down, his father popped up. "Thank you, thank you, Mr. O'Neill! Now may the father of the bride say a few words?"

Clearly interrupted mid-speech, Murph grinned and sat down with a "Love you, boss."

Richard talked about the long-ago summer when a teenage Adonis named Sandy Rodriguez came to work for his family in Maine. "Of course, our Pammy was only a toddler then, so she doesn't remember him. Every gal in our little town spent those two months swooning over him. Even our Ava," he added, winking at his eldest daughter. Finally, he ended with, "My dear Pam, light of our lives and beloved by all. Your mother would be so proud to see the amazing woman you are. You are so like her in temperament and beauty. She would have been pleased as punch to see the beautiful garden you've created in her memory. You're a lucky man, Sandy Rodriguez. Take care of her, and I wish you both all the happiness in the world."

A few more people spoke, including Gail and Raffi, Sandy's brother. In the growing twilight, dinner ended and the band began playing. People rose and milled about the barn and yard, both festooned with twinkle lights.

"Another great Morgan party," Kyle said as he found Rich by the bar.

Rich grinned. "Yup. They know how to do it."

"You next?" Kyle gazed across the barn to where his wife sat with Karen.

"Not without a miracle."

"She's crazy about you, man. She's just gotta heal and maybe get used to the new normal. What's the story anyway? Any progress?"

"You'd know better than I. She speaks to Harriet."

"Give it time. Give it time."

Kiki Bloom danced up to the two men and held out her hand to Kyle. "What d'ya say? How about a dance—doc to doc?"

Kyle gave her a look. "Won't your suitors mind?"

Kiki gazed over to spy Coop Merrick dancing with Milly Rodriguez. The farm's resident veterinarian had also been flirting shamelessly with Murph and a number of other local guys.

"I'm a free agent and proud of it, babe," she said, winking at Rich as she dragged Kyle onto the dance floor. "I'll be back for you later, Morgan," she added, pointing at Rich.

"Looks like our doc has had a bit too much to drink," Lucy said, coming to stand beside him.

Rich laughed. "Or she's just being Kiki."

His stepmother laughed. "That too. You having fun?"

"It's a nice party. You guys did great."

"But?"

"But if I had my druthers, I'd be home nursing a beer and watching the Red Sox. Don't get me wrong, I love my sister. Just not in a partying mood."

"Well, you better get in one!" his father said, strolling up with Ben and Leonora.

"Oh hell! Enough is enough," Rich said marching off.

Richard looked at Lucy. "What's put a bee in his bonnet?"

She smiled, taking his arm. "Not sure, but given the direction he's headed, I'd say it has something to do with a certain Ms. Miller."

"Well, good! 'Bout time. Now come dance with me, sweetheart."

CHAPTER 40

Harriet had stepped away leaving Karen seated by herself. *Now's my chance*, Rich thought and started toward her. When Karen spied him, she sat up, straightening her back. "Nice party."

"I came to see if you wanted to dance."

"Do I look like I can dance?"

"As a matter of fact, you do," he replied just as the band began to play Sam Cooke's "What a Wonderful World."

Before she could protest, Karen found herself being lifted and held tight, his strong arms keeping her several inches from the floor. Rich was almost a foot taller and now held her chest to chest. He could feel her heart beating as he gazed down to find her lips pursed and her eyes sparkling with surprise.

"This is ridiculous! I'm too heavy. After your operation, you shouldn't be lifting deadweight! Put me down this instant!"

"Nope. And don't worry about me. You're lighter than a file box, and I lift those all day long."

"Ha-ha. This is embarrassing. Bring me back to my seat. Now!"

"Nope," he said, swirling her around, his strong arms caressing her as they moved cheek to cheek.

When she looked up, his green eyes were soft, his feelings unmistakable. "You know how I feel."

"Don't care. I love you, and I'm going to dance with you."

"Just one dance," she said. Her arms circled his shoulders and she rested her head on his chest, his nearness suffusing her with warmth. How she loved his lean body, his scent of musk and spices, his gentle touch even as he held her tight. Karen closed her eyes. *Just one dance. Let me feel his love for just one dance.*

"Will you look at that," Richard said as he and Lucy danced by.

"Fingers crossed," Lucy said, as she caught Rich's eye and winked.

But it wasn't just one dance. Strains of Sinatra's "The Way You Look Tonight" began, and Rich held fast, praying that she wouldn't resist. He smiled, gratified as he felt her body melt into his.

Karen let out a deep sigh. *If I could stay here, in his arms, I know everything will be all right. This is the only place where I feel like myself.*

Rich felt her relax and held tighter. He decided to risk it and planted a soft kiss on her forehead. "Doing okay?" he said.

"Mm," she murmured, nestling closer. As the music went on, she gave herself over to its soft melody, wishing it could go on forever. She looked up and before she knew what she was doing, her lips found his.

Surprised, Rich returned the kiss, tentatively, gently so as not to spook her. As their tongues found each other, he held her tighter.

Karen felt him grow hard against her tummy, and she smiled, breaking the kiss and nuzzling his neck. "This could be very awkward for you, Mr. Morgan."

He chuckled. "Do you think I give a shit? As long as I can hold you like this, I don't care who notices my hard-on."

She grinned, gazing into his soft hazel eyes, her blue eyes sparkling with mischief. In that instant, the Karen he knew before her accident appeared.

"You know how much I want you right now, babe?"

"My, my, such language, Mr. Morgan. Why, I'm tempted to...oh!" Karen blanched, her eyes registering surprise.

"What is it? What's wrong?" he said.

"I thought I...I mean just now, it was as if...my leg. No, that's ridiculous. I'm tired, Rich. Can you bring me back to my seat, please?"

Rich reached down to cradle her in his arms, then carried her off the dance floor. Several people noticed the abrupt end to their dancing, including her parents. When they reached the table, he set her down, then knelt in front of her, knowing he only had seconds before her mother would be hovering.

"Tell me. You felt something, didn't you?"

Karen grabbed his sleeve. "Don't say anything. Please, Rich. Not until I'm sure. Not until I feel it again."

"But why?" he asked as Faith Miller came from behind.

"Baby, what's wrong? Are you okay?" she asked. "I knew this was too much for you."

Frowning, Karen raised her hands. "I'm fine, Mother. Just tired. I'm ready whenever someone can take me home."

Rich stood up. "I'll take you. Where's the wheelchair?"

Faith shook her head. "Absolutely not. This is your sister's wedding. You can't leave. Rex

and I will take her. Stay with her while I grab him."

Rich carried her to the car, her body rigid now, the earlier softness a distance memory. As he settled her in, he whispered, "I'm coming out to see you tomorrow," and quickly withdrew before she could say no.

ALL THE WAY HOME, HER MOTHER FUSSED AND FRETTED, BUT KAREN SAT quietly in the backseat, saying little except to assure them that she was okay.

"Leave her alone, Mama," Rex said as they drove through town. "She's tired, that's all."

Not tired. Hopeful, Karen thought, smiling as she caught her father's eye in the rearview mirror. They exchanged knowing looks, and he began to whistle.

"Rex, please!" Faith said. "I'm getting a headache, and I'm certain this is not the time for gaiety."

Ignoring his wife, he continued, strains of "Old Time Rock and Roll" filling the car.

CHAPTER 41

"She's a bitch and a terrible vet!" Weezie said. She stood at the dining room buffet, scooping scrambled eggs onto her plate. She then grabbed two slices of toast and bacon and plunked down in her chair.

Richard put his finger to his lips. "Hush, baby. We have guests. What will your aunt and uncle think?" Thus far, he, Rich, and Weezie were the only ones at the table

"Wouldn't be a typical day on the ranch if there weren't a few fireworks," Ben Morgan Senior said, grinning as he stepped in from the hall.

"Well, at least Leonora and Lucy went to town," Richard said. "What'll you have? If you don't see something you like, Callie can whip up most anything."

"This looks perfect," his brother said, grabbing a plate.

Callie poked her head in to ask if he wanted coffee, then disappeared.

Rich watched his sister, her face red as a beet as she pouted at the far end of the table. "We can't fire someone just because she's your rival for the affections of the handsome village smithy."

"Ha-ha. That's not it at all! You come down and watch her

someday. She's terrible with the horses. She spooks them. Every time she goes near them, either Gus, Dennis, or I have to be there."

"They don't know her, baby. They'll get used to her."

Eyes blazing, she looked up at her father. "Dad, I am not a baby. Did you hear what I said? She spooks them! Plus she doesn't know what she's doing. The difference between her and Kyle is night and day."

As Weezie's attention turned to her breakfast, Richard winked at Rich. "How about this? I will have a confidential conversation with Kyle. Ask him to stop in for a few days to work on something special. We'll dream up a plan that allows him to observe our Dr. Bloom in action. I'm assuming his professional opinion will satisfy you?"

"Humph!" Weezie said.

"Well, that's it for me. I'm taking off," Rich said.

"Where you headed, son?"

"Land's End, then home to collect some papers I forgot. I'll be back in the office by midafternoon. Ben it's been great to see you. I'll be at the farewell dinner tonight."

"Good on ya," his uncle said.

Richard clapped his hands. "That's it—Land's End! I'll offer Kiki's services to Faith and Rex. They can give us some feedback."

Rich gave him a look. "That's not in her contract Dad. She a doctor. You can't just pass her around like a piece of farm equipment. She'll balk, and I wouldn't blame her."

Richard grinned, winking at his brother. "Ah, my boy—you underestimate your father's powers of persuasion."

Rich rolled his eyes. "Well, don't come to me when she slaps you with a lawsuit or quits."

"Quitting would be great!" Weezie said, waving as he headed for the door.

FAITH MET HIM AT THE KITCHEN DOOR. "WE WERE SO GLAD TO GET your call this morning. You're good to come out. We're thrilled she didn't say no. I've got a million chores after taking yesterday off, and Rex is out straight. We tried to find someone to keep her company, but Sundays are hard."

"I'm happy to do it," Rich said. "Is she in the sunporch?"

She nodded. "Go on back. She's expecting you."

He found Karen reading a novel when he stepped into the sun-filled space.

"Hey," she said, patting the sofa cushion beside her.

"Haven't changed your mind?"

"No, have you?"

"Never." He leaned over and kissed her cheek.

Karen sighed, moving to rest her head against his shoulder. "I'm glad you're here."

"Me too."

They sat holding hands and talking. He told her about his father's plan to have them secretly assess Kiki Bloom's veterinary skills, which made her laugh. He loved her deep throaty laugh. It had been too long.

After an hour, he said, "Can I get you something? A drink or some food?"

"No, but I want to tell you something." She turned to face him, taking both his hands in hers.

"Of course. Shoot." Her hands were like ice. Instinctively, he began massaging them, trying to pass his warmth and strength to her fragile body.

For a moment, she sat silent, enjoying his touch. She had been cold for so long. Despite his mild-mannered nature, Rich radiated heat. *And passion*, she thought, giving him a soft smile. "You were right last night when we were dancing... I mean, if you could call that dancing with you twirling me around like a rag doll? As I said I...I did feel something...in my right leg."

"That's good news, right?"

She nodded. "And I've been trying to move it. It hurts, but I can move it a few inches."

"Have you called Janice?"

"It's Sunday. Physical therapists don't work today."

"I bet they do, and I bet she'd want to hear from you."

Karen shrugged, withdrawing her hands and gazing up at him shyly. "Janice is okay, but I'd rather work with you."

"I'm flattered, sweetie, but I wouldn't know where to begin. I might...we might do something that would hurt you. Even set you back?"

For a second her blue eyes flashed fire and her mouth screwed up in a pout. "I don't care."

"Well, I do."

"Please Rich! We can be careful. Just tiny steps."

Eyes wide in astonishment, he looked at her. "Steps? Isn't that a little ambitious?"

"At the first sign of pain, I'll stop. Now stand up."

He gave her a look.

"Please?"

"Okay, but I'm holding on to you." He stood in front of her, noting her slender arms in a sleeveless eyelet top as she reached up to him. The blouse's first three buttons were undone, revealing her white lacy bra and the soft curves of her breasts. Her denim capris hung on her thin frame and looked three sizes too big.

He grasped her gently just under her arms and lifted her feather-light body so she dangled several inches from the floor. Karen draped her arms around his neck and kissed him. He returned the kiss, his tongue parting her lips as hers teased and tickled him. She felt his arousal and grinned. "Whoa, boy, first things first."

"I couldn't agree more, even if some parts of my anatomy are not cooperating. You okay?"

She nodded. "Now lower me down slowly. I'll tell you if I'm not okay."

He complied, holding tight as her bare feet brushed the sisal rug. "Okay?"

"Yup. Now I want to try to stand and put my weight on it. Ouch!"

Instantly, he lifted her. "Oh geez, you all right?"

"I'm fine. The stupid brace twisted and pinched me, that's all."

"But you felt the pinch. That's a good sign, isn't it?" He was rewarded with a beautiful smile. *Oh, how I've missed that smile*, he thought.

"A very good sign. Now set me down again."

He held her by the waist as she stood, her weight distributed on both legs. "How's it feel?"

"Like I'm Frankenstein's monster figuring out how to walk for the first time."

He laughed. "Well, you don't look like a monster. In fact, you look as pretty as you've ever looked."

"Liar. Now come on, step back a little." She pushed him away, grasping hold of his forearms.

"I'm not sure this is a good idea."

"Well, I am," she said, stepping forward with her left leg, then dragging the right into alignment. "Okay...now comes the real test."

Fingers dug into his arms, she pursed her lips, took a deep breath, and lifted her right leg inching it forward. It was an awkward movement that threw her off balance. He reached around and grasped her arms, holding her steady. When Rich looked down, there were tears in her eyes. "Oh geez, this is hurting you, isn't it? We should stop."

In response, she stood up straighter and brought her left leg forward. "It hurts like hell, but I don't care. Come on, let's take a few more steps."

"Only a few, and then you're resting."

Slowly, they crossed the narrow sunporch until his back rested against the window frame. He leaned over and kissed her forehead. "You did it."

"Yes," she said as she collapsed into his arms, a weary smile on her face. "Thank you."

She closed her eyes and went limp. Afraid she'd fainted, he cradled her in his arms and carried her back to the sofa. Gently laying her down, he knelt on the floor. "Good girl," he said, kissing. "Rest now."

Karen opened her eyes, gave him a dreamy smile, and said, "Good idea," and promptly fell asleep.

He sat beside her for a while, then wrote a note saying he'd stop by later.

It's a start, he thought, grinning as he drove down the farm's long drive. *Let's hope it's a healthy one.*

CHAPTER 42

In between work for Morgan Enterprises, the farm and winery, Rich managed to break away for several hours every day to visit with Karen. As the days went on, she grew stronger. They let Janice in on their secret and she urged them to contact Dr. Cote, but Karen wanted to wait a few more days. At the end of the week, Janice told them, "You've made so much progress in such a short time. I can wait till Monday, then I have to update Dr. Cote. She'll probably want to see you immediately."

"Sunday's my mom's birthday. I thought we'd surprise them and then the world can know."

The therapist shook her head, stuffing equipment into her bag. "I could lose my job for this."

Karen reached over and squeezed her arm. "Thanks, Janice!"

After Janice departed, Rich sat beside her. "She gave you a workout today, didn't she? How are you feeling? Ready for a nap?"

"Truthfully, I'm ready to throw off this brace and have wild, dirty sex."

He laughed, kissing her forehead. "I'm not even sure what that is."

She gave him a mischievous look "Well, as soon as this comes off, I'll show you." She ran her hand up his thigh, caressing him. "Come to think of it, I could give *you* wild, dirty sex right now."

He smiled, taking hold of her hand, which had already succeeded in arousing him. "Tempting as that is, I just heard the back door slam. Not sure I'm ready to be that intimate with your parents."

"Your choice, babe," she said, her tone flippant as he brought her hand to his lips and kissed her palm.

"I've gotta go," he said. "We've got a meeting at the winery at six. What's tomorrow like for you?"

Karen gave him a look. "What do you think?"

"Well, I have an idea. I have to be at Morgan's Fire in the morning, but why don't I ask Callie to pack us a picnic? We could take one of the golf carts, if they'd be free, and head down to the Point. It's supposed to be a nice day."

"Perfect." She drew him close for a deep, searing kiss, her arms around his shoulders, breasts pressed against him.

Rich responded, lost in his desire for her, heedless of where they were. No telling what would have happened if Faith hadn't knocked on the door. "Hey, guys, can I come in?"

They broke apart, and Karen called, "Hi, Mom!"

Faith stepped into the room and looked from one to the other. "Am I interrupting?"

"Perfect timing as always, Mom," Karen said, leaning back on the sofa.

Red-faced, Rich stood, his sweatshirt held in front of him. "Not interrupting a thing. I was just leaving."

"Oh, I'm sorry," Faith said. "I can come back."

"No, really," he said. "I have to be at Morgan's Fire. I asked Karen if she might like to take a picnic to the Point tomorrow."

Faith clapped her hands. "What a lovely idea. Shall I pack you some sandwiches?"

"Thanks, but you're busy. I'll ask Callie to do it. She loves stuff like this. I did wonder if we could borrow one of the golf carts."

"Of course! I'll ask Brick to park one near the house tomorrow morning."

Karen cleared her throat. "What time will you be here?"

"Twelve thirty? Is that too late?"

"Perfect." She beckoned with her hands.

Rich bent over and kissed her cheek. "See you tomorrow, then."

"I'll walk you out, honey."

Faith followed him through the house and out to his car. "Thank you so much, Rich. I'm not sure what the future will bring, but your presence this past week has brought the color back to our baby's cheeks. Her spirits are so much better and her dad and I are so grateful."

"It's been my pleasure. I love her."

Faith nodded. "Yes, and she's crazy about you."

For a moment, his eyes reflected sadness. "She's got a tough road ahead. I'd just like to be here when and if she'll let me."

"That gate seems to have reopened," she said, hugging him. "And Rex and I couldn't be happier."

Rich returned her embrace, then hopped into the BMW. "See you tomorrow, then?"

"Absolutely! Have a great evening, sweetie."

CHAPTER 43

Shortly after noon Saturday, Rich and Karen set off for the Point in a Land's End golf cart. As they passed by the barn, they spied Kiki Brown examining one of the stable mares, a beautiful brown Arabian. "That's my Brandi," Karen said. "And she better know what she's doing."

"Is she okay?" Rich asked. "Brandi, I mean."

"A little colic, but she's fine. I think she misses me."

"I'm sure she does." He leaned closer and whispered, "And what about Dr. Bloom? Does she appear to be passing muster?"

"She's terrific. I mean, she's not your cousin Kyle, but that's just 'cause he knows the horses really well. But Kiki knows what she's doing, according to Brick and my dad."

"Of course she does," Rich said, waving at the vet as she stood up to stretch. "This is about my spoiled baby sister and her crush on Coop Merrick. From what my brother-in-law Tim says, Coop hasn't had many girlfriends, so he must be reeling with all this attention."

Karen waved her hand. "Small-town-itis. They'll sort it out. They always do."

A hot day, there was a gentle breeze as the cart climbed the knoll leading to the area the locals called the Point or the Nubble. A huge rock jutted out where land met the water, but further inland, there were a number of grassy spots, some sheltered from the wind. "What's your pleasure, milady?" he asked. "Do you have a favorite spot?"

Karen pointed eastward. "Let's check out Dilly's."

"Dilly's?" he asked, eying her.

"That's right. You're not a local."

Rich laughed. "Unless you count the past two years."

"Buddy, you're not a local till you've been around at least ten, maybe fifteen years, and even then you're considered a newcomer local. Here we are!"

He drove between two outcroppings into a boulder-lined meadow, mowed and green. Flowers grew along the perimeter, a riot of color. Lupines, hollyhocks, daisies, day lilies, wild irises and a host of others in wild profusion.

Rich whistled. "Wow!"

"Welcome to Dilly's Corner. It's named for my great grandma, my mom's grandmother. Legend has it that she had farm laborers haul in all these huge stones. She then planted the flowers and shrubs so she could have a secluded private place."

"It's beautiful. And so are you," he said, reaching over, his fingers caressing her cheek.

Karen smiled, patting his knee. "Flattery will get you everywhere, but let's get settled first, okay?"

"You stay put till I spread blankets and chairs and set up the picnic." He kissed her lightly, then hopped off the cart.

Happier than she'd been in many weeks, Karen watched him. *He is the one,* she told herself. *I've never felt like this about any man, even my former fiancés.* After a few minutes, she slid to the edge of her seat, grasped the cart's frame, and stood on wobbly legs.

Rich spied her and put up his hand. "Wait, please! I'll be right there."

"Why don't I try to come to you?"

"Absolutely not! The ground's uneven, and if you fall, you could send yourself back to square one."

"What a cheerful thought. All right, then, come get me, gorgeous."

She held out her arms, and he hurried to her side, slipping his arm around her waist. "I can carry you?"

"Nope, I'm walking. Let's go."

Slowly, they made their way the ten feet to where he'd set up. "Chair or blanket?" he asked.

"Blanket, please."

Gently he set her down, and Karen pulled herself upright.

"Good?"

She smiled. "Perfect."

"Something to drink? Callie's got iced tea, water, lemonade, and white wine."

"I'd actually love wine," she said, as she began unstrapping her brace.

Aghast, Rich stared at her. "What are you doing?"

"Getting comfortable. We're not walking around, and I want to be comfortable. I don't wear this in bed, you know." She undid the final strap and gently lifted her leg, throwing the brace to the side.

"What would Dr. Cote say about that?"

"I don't give a shit. Now, wine, please!"

THEY SAT SIDE BY SIDE, SIPPING THEIR WINE IN COMPANIONABLE SILENCE, enjoying the peace and quiet. "This is nice," she purred, snuggling against him.

Rich reached around to cradle her back. "Sure is. You sure you're okay without the brace?"

"I almost feel like I'm whole right now."

"You *are* whole, babe. You're making great progress."

"Then kiss me as if I'm whole, not an invalid."

Rich gazed down to find her blue eyes beseeching him. "Not sure what that means," he lied, hand softly cupping her chin.

Karen reached up, arms around his neck as she leaned back on the blanket and pulled him with her. "Oh yes, you do. Kiss me like you want to take this the whole way, not just a hi and goodbye."

He raised one eyebrow, smiling as he allowed himself to be drawn closer. "Hi and goodbye, huh? Okay...you did ask."

"Yes, I did," she said, lips finding his, her tongue teasing, delving and begging for more.

Rich slipped his hand under her shirt, caressing her glorious breasts. Karen slipped out of blouse and bra, casting them aside with a grin.

"You are a wicked woman, aren't you?"

"Betta believe it," she said, voice husky as her hand moved down his chest to his belly, her lips and tongue tracing a sensual path down his neck. As she began fondling and stroking his cock through his khaki shorts, Rich moaned. "Geez, babe, is this a good idea?"

She gave him a wicked look. "The best," she said as her hand traveled down his leg, then back up under the hem. "Isn't it time these shorts came off?"

"Ladies first," he said, coming up on one elbow to help her slip out of her denim capris and lacy panties. "Oh God, baby, you are so beautiful."

"Come on, champ," she whispered, her hands tugging at his shorts.

"This is against my better judgment, but I'm not sure I can wrestle the beast back into its cage. You sure you're okay?"

"Perfect," she said as she guided his hand between her legs.

As his fingers touched her warm, wet depths, Rich captured her lips again, every move designed to express his love and fierce longing. She had released his cock and was driving him blind with her caresses. Karen broke free of his lips and whispered, "Please, I need you now."

Suddenly, he sat up. "Shit, no condom!"

"You didn't bring one?"

"Well, no... I never imagined this would... Shit."

"No worries!" She reached over and grabbed her capris, extracting a condom from the back pocket. "Voila!"

Rich grinned. "How did you...? Do I even want to know?"

"I'll tell you later. Now, let's get this on!" After she slipped the condom on, Karen melted into the curve of his body, one hand working its magic as she caressed him.

Breathless, he took first one, then the other perfect breast in his mouth, tongue circling as he teased her nipples to quivering peaks of sensation. Karen moaned, her body crushing against him.

"Are you sure? Am I hurting you?" he whispered.

"Surer than I've ever been." Her hips moved against him in desperate rhythm. "Take me now, before I go completely insane."

Ascertaining that she was okay, Rich moved between her legs, his fingers slipping out as his cock found her white-hot center. Tentative and careful, he entered her, then gasped as she rose to meet him, taking him deeper and deeper with each explosive thrust.

"Oh sweetie, you are incredible," he whispered, his last coherent thought as they moved in exquisite harmony, soaring to shuddering ecstasy.

Bodies slick with sweat, they relaxed into each other. Tears sprang to Karen's eyes as she felt herself flooded with uncontrollable joy. As her hand reached up to caress his cheek, Rich spied the tears.

"Oh my God, have I hurt you?"

She shook her head, unable to speak.

"Oh, Karen, I'm sorry. We never should have... If you're hurt, I'll never forgive myself."

In answer, she pulled him down, kissing him deeply, her tongue exploring, teasing. When she broke free, she was smiling. "I am the polar opposite of hurt. I feel great, no pain, but more importantly, I'm happy. I'm truly happy."

Rich smiled. "I love you."

"And I love you," she said, kissing him lightly. "For the first time in my life, I know how that feels."

He twirled a finger around a lock of her hair. "Not gonna change your mind, are you?"

"Never I... Do you hear that? Shit! I hear voices." Wild-eyed, Karen grabbed for her shirt.

"Oh boy," he said, hurriedly pulling on his shorts and shirt, then helping her into her clothes.

Karen was just buttoning her blouse when a family of four, two children and their parents, appeared on bikes at the edge of the field. "Hi," the dad called. "Great spot for a picnic! Mind if we join you?" If he was aware of what they'd just been up to, he gave no indication.

The four were strangers. Ordinarily, Karen would have firmly but politely informed them that this was private property and directed them to one of the public picnic spots on the water side of the Loop Trail. While the Millers were not territorial, they usually restricted public use of Land's End acreage because of liability and the nuisance of picking up after people. At this moment, in the afterglow of their lovemaking, she didn't care.

"Of course, welcome to Dilly's Corner!"

The man's wife tapped him on the shoulder, smiling at Karen and Rich. "Thanks, but Ken, remember? The kids want to eat at the Point where they can see the ocean."

"It's a bay, actually," Karen said. "Are you from around here?"

"Boston," Ken said. "Visiting friends. Best sightseeing we've ever had. Beautiful spot."

"Yes, it is," Rich said, standing now, hands on hips.

Ken shrugged. "Well, you heard the boss. I guess we're eating by the water. Enjoy!"

As the four pedaled off between the boulders, Rich and Karen looked at each other and burst into peals of laughter. "Good thing they didn't come ten minutes earlier. Talk about sightseeing!" He knelt down beside her and grabbed the basket. "You hungry?"

"Starved! And after lunch, I'd like to try a tiny walk around without the brace."

"Are you sure?"

She leaned against him, sinking into the warmth of his embrace. "As sure as I am that I love you. Do you promise you'll be there tomorrow?" she asked, referring to her mother's birthday dinner.

"If it's okay with everyone."

"Of course it is."

"Then I'll be there. Now let's see what Callie's packed for us."

CHAPTER 44

As promised, Rich arrived at Land's End at five thirty the following evening. Before heading to the Millers', he had stopped at Morgan's Fire, then done errands in town. He was way behind at work, but he didn't care. He would do anything for Karen. Everything else paled in comparison.

They sat at the long wooden table in the garden, all fourteen of them. Faith and Rex were at either end flanked by Brick and his family, Rex Junior, Jonas, Tim and Gail, and Karen and Rich. The table groaned with food. Tim, a lobsterman, had brought enough lobsters to feed an army, and they were placed in huge bowls along the middle of the table where people grabbed them, tied on bibs, and dug in. Gail and Susie, Brick's wife, had made potato salad, green salad, and several pasta salads. Rich had been tasked with bringing crusty sourdough bread from the Moon and Stars Bakery in town. Susie and her kids Amy and Bobby made the birthday cake now hidden in a cool spot on the sunporch.

"Not enough food here," Jonas said as he grabbed his second lobster. "I'll miss this out west."

"When are you heading back?" Rich asked as he felt Karen's touch on his thigh. As her fingers made their way toward his groin, he reached down and grasped her hand. *That's all I need right now!*

"Tomorrow. Plane arrives in the morning. I should be there now, but after the wedding, I asked to stay for this, and you know Spark. He never says no."

His father grinned. "I expect your Mr. Foster says no when needed in business. He didn't get to be a billionaire without saying no from time to time."

Rich laughed. "No doubt you're right. He is sure generous with his wealth, isn't he?"

"You have no idea," Jonas said. "He's one of the top philanthropists on the West Coast, maybe the country or the world."

"I love Spark," Karen said dreamily. "That was the high point in our trip to Saguaro, staying at the Foster mansion."

"Not all the lovely parties and celebrations?" her mother asked, smiling as she watched her daughter. *Thank God for Rich Morgan, a true miracle worker*, she mused.

"Oh, those too," she said, slipping her hand under the table again.

Rich grabbed hold, turning to smile at her. Thoughts of the previous day in Dilly's Corner and her electric touch were enough to turn him rock hard, his breath quickening. As he shifted his napkin to cover his lap, he caught her mischievous grin.

Karen leaned over, whispering, "Remember, right after dessert."

Rich squeezed her hand. "All set."

After several choruses of "Happy Birthday," Susie set a long, flat sheet cake in front of Faith. It was covered in green frosting and decorated with a miniature barn, silo, and farm animals. "We did the animals," Bobby said, peeking out from behind his mother.

Faith winked at him. "Oh, precious, what a beautiful job you did!"

"Me too, Grandma," Amy said, running to grab her grandmother's waist.

Tears sprang to Faith eyes as she hugged her grandchildren. "What a special, special birthday this is. I love you all so much!"

A large bucket of ice cream and scoop in hand, Gail followed Betsy around as she set plates of cake in front of each person. When she reached her brother, whom she had been sitting beside, Gail leaned closer and whispered, "Better watch that hanky-panky. I'm not the only one who's noticed."

Startled Rich gazed to find his sister smiling. He raised his hand, saying "No thanks," as she offered him a scoop of vanilla ice cream.

"You sure?" Gail asked, grinning.

He gave her a look. "Move along, sis." This was such a departure for him, a leading role in the farcical situation created by Karen's roving hands. The quiet one he usually took a back seat to any family shenanigans. Steady, sensible Rich, a port in the storm when family emotions ran high. *Now here I am in the middle of the shenanigans, and there's not a damn thing I can do about it,* he thought. *But truth be told, I don't care. This is her moment, or will be soon.*

CAKE AND ICE CREAM GONE, DINERS SAT BACK, ENJOYING COFFEE, TEA, or other drinks. As several people made movements to rise, Karen called out, "Wait! Everyone stay seated. Please!" Startled eyes looked down the table at her. In answer, she reached up. Rich stood, stooping to cradle her in his arms. They had planned it all out. He would set her down by the terrace wall and she would get her balance.

As her daughter's feet touched the ground, Faith called out. "Oh, honey, what are you doing?"

Karen caught hold of Rich's arm to steady herself and raised her other hand. "Please, Mama, hush! I'm fine."

As her family watched, their eyes wide, jaws dropped, Karen pushed away from the wall and began a slow, stilted walk toward the table and her mother. Rich stayed close, his arm out, ready to catch her if she faltered, but she didn't. Lips pursed, jaw set, Karen crossed the distance until she stood in front of her mother. "Happy birthday, Mama!" she said as she fell into Faith's arms.

Everyone rose, clapping, cheering, and some crying. Rex flew to the end of the table and embraced her, followed by her brothers. When the clamor died down, Faith said, "How?" to her daughter who now sat in her lap.

"Practice, lots of practice. This guy's been helping me," she added, gazing up at Rich. "I couldn't have done it without him and Janice."

Faith stared at her. "Janice knew about this and didn't tell us?"

"I swore her to secrecy. She plans to communicate with Dr. Cote tomorrow."

Faith clapped. "Can't wait to hear what she says at your appointment Tuesday."

"Rich is taking me," Karen said quietly, reaching up to take his hand.

Her face registered disappointment, but then Faith smiled at her daughter, then Rich. "Of course, sweetie, as he should."

When the evening was over, Rich carried her inside and gently set her on the sofa in the sunroom. "Congratulations, baby," he said, kissing her forehead, then moving down to capture her full rosy lips for a good-night kiss.

"We did it."

"*You* did it."

"Will I see you tomorrow?"

"Probably not. I owe my dad a long day's work, and I have errands and a bunch of meetings."

She made a pouty face, then smiled. "Well, I'll have you all to myself Tuesday."

"Absolutely. You okay if I go? Will the gang help you to bed?"

"No prob, but I want one more real kiss, not a friendly 'hi, how are you' kiss." Her arms circled his neck, and he allowed her to draw him close.

By the time he broke away, the world was spinning. She reached down to stroke his hard cock and grinned. "Why, Mr. Morgan, do you want more?"

"You know I do, so I'm gonna take off before your brothers find us in a compromising position."

"Too bad for them."

"It would be too bad for me, I fear." He kissed the tip of her nose, then stood up. "Fortunately, I have my jacket," he said, holding it in front of him.

She shrugged. "As far as I'm concerned, they can see you hard and panting. Not like they haven't been there plenty themselves."

Rich chuckled. "Good night."

"Night, Tiger," she said, smiling up at him with tired eyes. "Thank you for tonight."

"My pleasure. I love you," he said. "Don't push too much tomorrow."

"Love you too."

CHAPTER 45

Monday was a blur of meetings and phone calls, but Rich made time to run into the village to Cove Jewelers. Small box in hand, he exited the shop, a huge shit-eating grin on his face, and ran straight into Sandy, his brother-in-law.

"Hey, Rich, where's the fire? Jewelers? Buying something special?"

Rich hesitated, then decided he could use a second opinion. "Can you keep a secret?"

"I'm the soul of discretion, buddy. No one gets a secret out of me."

"Not even my sister?"

"Hmm... For how long?"

"Just till tomorrow night."

"Even though we swore to be open and honest with each other, I'm sure one day won't hurt."

"Okay, come back inside." He pulled Sandy into the jewelers, checked the front window for passersby, then he reached into his pocket and pulled out the blue velvet box. He opened it to reveal an exquisite diamond set with sapphires on each side. "What do you think?"

Sandy whistled. "I assume this is for Karen Miller?"

Rich nodded.

Sandy slapped him on the back. "She's gonna love it, man."

"That's what I think," Rich said. "Thanks, and remember, mum's the word."

"No prob, bro."

The two men parted company, and Rich hopped into his car, still smiling as he headed back to the farm. He spent three hours in his office before he felt caught up. Before he departed for home, he called the Grille in town and ordered dinner, mushroom ravioli, and a large salad. He decided it would be best to avoid his father, who could always read his mood, so he skirted the main house on his way to his car. He almost made it.

"Hey, son!" Richard called from the front porch where he and Lucy sat sipping wine. "Come have a drink before you go."

"Thanks, Dad, but I just ordered dinner from the Grille, and I don't want it to get cold."

"Dinner? You could've eaten with us."

"Want to have an early night."

"Something wrong?"

"Not at all," Rich said, gazing at Lucy, his eyes pleading for help.

"Let him go, dear," she said, waving at Rich.

As the BMW headed down the drive, Richard turned to her. "Something's up with that boy."

She reached over and took his hand, squeezing gently. "Looks like a good something."

"Oh?"

"He looked happy, don't you think?"

"Hmm... Could it be the pretty Ms. Miller?"

She laughed. "We'll just have to wait and see, nosey Parker."

CHAPTER 46

Dr. Cote completed her examination and helped Karen to sit up. Rich sat beside her after Karen had insisted that he stay.

"Let's just get this back on," the physician said, grabbing the brace from the adjacent table.

"I thought I'd be done with that," Karen said.

Gretchen Cote smiled, her eyes kind, hand resting on Karen's knee. "Not quite yet. You've made great progress, but the leg and hip still need support."

Karen shook her head, tears threatening to fall. "But I...we've worked so hard. I don't want... I can't."

"I understand your disappointment, but it won't be forever. We can't take the chance of you injuring the hip." As she spoke, Dr. Cote grabbed a tissue box from the table and handed it to Karen. "I'm going to step out and gather some materials. I also want to get the schedule for the follow-up tests you'll need next week. Now that you have feeling, I want to proceed somewhat differently. Will you excuse me?"

When the door closed, Rich turned to see tears streaming down Karen's cheeks. "Hey, hey, sweetie. This is good news."

More head shaking. "No, it's not! I want to be done! I want... I want to...so we can get on with our lives. You shouldn't be with a cripple. Why did I ever let my guard down and start this up again?"

Surprised at her torrent of emotions, Rich wondered if it was lack of sleep. Before things degenerated further, he decided it was time. He slipped from his chair and knelt beside her. "Hey, sweetie, everything's going to be fine. We're going to be fine, promise." He reached into his pocket and drew out the tiny velvet box. "I was going to do this tonight at dinner, but maybe now is better."

Karen sniffled, wiping tears away with a tissue as she gazed into his eyes. "What are you doing?"

He smiled. "I'm on my knee, as you can see, because I have a very important question to ask you."

Eyes big as saucers, tears forgotten, she said, "What question?"

"I love you, Karen Miller. I've loved you since the first day we met. I never thought a beautiful woman like you could love a dullard like me."

"You aren't dull!"

He shrugged. "Maybe, maybe not. Anyway, I love you and I don't want to spend another minute or day without you. I need you in my life as much as I need air to breathe."

"Yes," she said softly.

"I haven't asked you yet."

"But I know what you're going to ask, and the answer is yes."

"Will you please let me ask first?

"Okay, but hurry up. Dr. Cote will be back soon!"

"Will you marry me and make me the happiest man in the world?"

"Yes," she said, collapsing into his arms. "Yes, yes, yes! If you're crazy enough to ask me, my answer is yes!"

"Oh, baby, I love you."

"I love you too," she said as his lips captured hers for a deep, smoldering kiss.

That was how Dr. Cote found them several minutes later. "Oh, shall I come back?" she asked, smiling even as her gaze traveled over the entwined bodies, checking to see if her patient was safe.

Karen gazed up, her eyes sparkling with light. "We're getting married!"

"Well, congratulations. Now, can you please get up? That position looks awkward and dangerous. We want you healed and ready to walk down the aisle."

Rich stood and picked Karen up, setting her in the chair. He then met Dr. Cote's gaze and shrugged. "Seemed like the right moment."

The physician smiled. "The right moment... That's all that matters. I wish you both such joy and happiness."

Updates about future releases, please visit my AUTHOR WEBSITE and sign up for my Newsletter and Follow me on BookBub!

Please read on for chapters from *Lolly's Wish!*

LOLLY'S WISH

Chapter I

"I'm a hopeless case, so don't bother trying to cheer me up," Lolly said to her business partner as they sorted a shipment of books.

Hands on hips, Lucy Morgan gazed at stacks of floor-to-ceiling boxes and shook her head. "We really have to get a bigger office. This is ridiculous. And you are not a hopeless case. Not by a long shot."

The two women owned a successful mail-order book business, Merlin's Closet, specializing in children's books. In addition to the mail order, they ran popular bookfairs in local towns and schools. For the past two years, they'd added adult mysteries to their catalogue and website, and their business had exploded.

"Never mind a bigger office," Lolly said. "We need more help."

"Where would we fit another person in this rabbit warren?"

"Back to my pathetic life. You have to admit I behaved like a big girl through the wedding."

"Yes, you did. Even Richard remarked on your grace and generosity under trying circumstances."

Lucy's stepdaughter, Pam Morgan, had recently wed Sandy Rodriguez, Lolly's ex-husband. Theirs had been an acrimonious divorce, with years of hurt and unresolved emotions.

The wedding had been at Morgan's Fire, the farm Lucy's husband, Richard, had created on the outskirts of Horseshoe Crab Cove. The Merlin's Closet office was located in town, on the second floor above Cove Toys and Games. They tried to process all books through the office, but recently moved overflow shipments to one of the farm barns.

"The mindfulness helps," Lolly said, referring to an eight-week course she'd recently completed at Cove Yoga Center. "There was so much pain, you know?"

Her friend nodded.

"I've been mostly successful in letting go. Wasn't Maisie the cutest flower girl?"

"She sure was. All the kids did great."

Lolly's eyes misted, and she set down a stack of mysteries. "Now there's my next hurdle."

"Oh?"

"Maisie's new mother."

"*You* are Maisie's mother, dearie. Nothing will ever change that."

"I know, but it's still hard thinking of them together, you know? Having fun on the weekends while I sit home alone or with Mother. As Mother likes to say—divorce is the gift that keeps on giving. Isn't that the truth?"

Lucy came to sit beside her. "I couldn't agree more. Divorce sucks."

Lolly put her head on her partner's shoulder. "You're one of the lucky ones. Not only is your Richard an amazing man, he's filthy rich to boot."

"Yes, he's a kind, lovely man, but there are lots more out there." After a painful divorce from her husband of eighteen years, Lucy had fallen in love with the wealthy businessman farmer and now lived at Morgan's Fire with Richard, her two teenagers, and several of her husband's adult offspring.

"Name me one."

"Well...we might have to go a little further afield than Horseshoe Crab Cove, but he's out there. I know he is!"

"Ever the optimist. At this point, I'm not even sure what I'd do with a man if I found one. I'm so out of practice in the dating game. Let's get lunch and come back to this mess with renewed vigor."

"Great idea. It's such a pretty day. How about we grab sandwiches from the Café and walk down to the garden?"

Lolly hopped up, brushing cardboard bits and dust from the front of her jeans. "Sounds like a plan!"

As the friends strolled down Main Street, they were a study in contrasts, Lucy tall and slender with sky-blue eyes and shoulder-length sandy hair, and Lolly, buxom and curvaceous, with thick raven hair and violet eyes.

"Maybe I should cut my hair in a bob like yours? What do you think?" Lolly asked as they neared the Cove Café.

Lucy smiled. "I think your hair is gorgeous just the way it is, but it's your decision."

Jack Faulkner passed the "Welcome to Horseshoe Crab Cove" sign and wondered if he'd made a mistake. Tired of the city, he'd volunteered to spend a few weeks, maybe longer, in the village of Horseshoe Crab Cove. There to assess the potential for development of a property in a prime location at the village's southwest corner, he'd left so much work behind, he'd go crazy trying to catch up. Was a few weeks in the country, even beautiful country like this, worth the aggravation?

As he drove into town, he searched the street for the Crab Café where he was to meet with Lindsay Barnes, the Realtor handling the Barnum property. Just as he spotted the café's sign, he also spied two beautiful women heading into the restaurant, one skinny, one not so much. As a heavy-set guy, Jack preferred a woman with curves, and this one was something! *Maybe this won't be so bad after all,* he thought, parking in a lot at the end of the street.

As he entered the café, he spied the two women at the counter waiting to order. Since no one had run up to greet him, he decided to make a couple of new friends. "Hi, ladies," he said, elbow resting on the counter as he leaned forward to address them both.

They turned as one. The slender one smiled, her blue eyes warm. "Hello." Her raven-haired companion just stared, her beautiful violet eyes curious.

"I don't suppose either of you know Lindsay Barnes? I'm supposed to meet her here."

"End of the counter, chatting with the waitress. You must be new in town. I'm Lucy Morgan, and this is my friend Lolly Rogers."

He grinned, extending his hand. "Jack Faulkner." They both shook his hand, but he only felt electricity when he and Lucy's companion touched. *Hmm...*

"Mr. Faulkner?" the woman from the end of the counter asked, stepping between Jack and his new friends.

He nodded.

"Lindsay Barnes. Welcome to Horseshoe Crab Cove."

"Hello, thanks for meeting me, Ms. Barnes," he said, extending his hand to the petite blonde in a red business suit, crisp white blouse, and five-inch heels. Even with the shoes, he towered over her. Early forties, he guessed. Her pixie haircut suited her, the gobs of makeup not so much. "These kind ladies had just pointed you out."

"Hey, gals," she said, giving Lucy and Lolly a quick glance before returning her green eyes to the handsome newcomer. "I see you've met our booksellers, two of the town's most successful businesswomen."

"Hardly," Lolly said.

Jack turned to the raven-haired beauty. "Oh? Where's your bookshop? I'd like to stop in and grab some reading material for my visit." The woman had the most exquisite violet eyes. *Liz Taylor has nothing on Lolly Rogers.*

"No shop, we're strictly mail order. Sorry." *You don't know how sorry I am!* she thought, weak-kneed as she conversed with the handsome stranger with broad shoulders, a stocky build and sandy hair. His wire-rimmed glasses accentuated his warm blue eyes.

Lucy smiled as she watched the interplay between her friend and the attractive stranger. "We sell children's books and a small catalog of mysteries, but Village Books is right down the street, and they have a great selection of all genres."

"Jack, why don't I find us a table?" Lindsay said, hand grazing his arm.

Ignoring the Realtor, he turned to Lolly. "Adult mysteries?"

She nodded. "We pride ourselves in finding authors of regional mysteries with a strong sense of place along with wonderful, intricate plotting." Lolly wondered if she might be babbling a bit.

He smiled, gaze lingering on Lolly. "My favorite kind. Might I get a catalog somewhere?"

Lolly blushed. "Well, we... I mean we don't... There are some upcoming bookfairs."

"I tell you what," Lucy said, reaching into her purse. "Here's our card. We're right up the street, second floor above Cove Toys and Games. We're usually in between ten and four, but I'd call ahead. We'd be happy to recommend a good mystery or two. If it's in stock, it's yours."

"Oh look, Jack!" Lindsay said. "A table has opened by the window. Shall we?" She took his arm.

Jack grinned, holding up the card as he allowed himself to be dragged away. "Thanks. I'll be in touch!"

Their sandwiches ready, the partners took their bags and made their way to the door. Lindsay had positioned Jack so that his back was to them, so he failed to notice their departure.

"Well, well, well," Lucy said as they stepped out. "That was interesting."

Lolly shrugged. "What are you talking about?"

Lucy paused on the sidewalk, laughing. "You know damn well what I'm talking about. Mr. Tall, Dark, and Handsome?"

Lolly smiled. "Not so tall, light hair, but you're right... Very handsome. Men like that like women like you and Lindsay Barnes, not dumpy old me."

"Don't be ridiculous. Jack Faulkner couldn't be less interested in Lindsay or me.

He only had eyes for you, my dear. Beautiful blue eyes, I might add."

"Just being polite. Now, let's go. I'm starving."

"If that was polite, I can't wait to see your Mr. Faulkner turn on the charm."

"He is not my Mr. Faulkner, and I doubt we'll ever see him again. I wonder why he's here anyway. What would he want with Lindsay? Why didn't we think to ask?"

"Hmm... If you're interested, I can tap into the town grapevine. I'm sure there'll be chatter by tonight."

"Ha-ha," Lolly said, smiling as she led the way into Laura's Community Garden. "There's a bench in the shade. Come on."

Chapter 2

Jack whistled as he and Lindsay stood on the porch of Barnum's Ledge, the three-story inn at the southwest corner of Horseshoe Crab Cove.

"Some view, isn't it?" she asked. In front of them, Mount Hope Bay sparkled. As far as the eye could see, blue waves crested white as the wind picked up.

"View's terrific, building will have to be razed, cottages too."

They had spent the last hour touring the property, which consisted of the huge Victorian main building, six guest cottages, two barns, and several smaller outbuildings. The Barnum family had moved away a decade earlier, leaving a caretaker who was tasked to maintain the place, but who had basically done nothing. When the disrepair came to the attention of the town manager, he contacted the Barnums, who were now spread out all over the country.

Finger to her lips, Lindsay assumed a pensive look. "Oh, I don't know. Surely some of the cottages can be salvaged, and with a good contractor, maybe the inn too? I know a few excellent contractors."

Jack smiled. "We'd bring our people in for this."

"Oh, well...of course," she said, not quite successful in keeping the pique from her voice. "So what's our next step?"

"I'll bring a team down to go over it. Should be able to get my people here tomorrow or the next day. Would you have any free time?"

She smiled, leaning into him. "For you, anytime." Lindsay had been flirting since they met in the Café, but Jack was definitely not interested. Still, it didn't hurt to play along if it meant a better sales price.

"Basically, we'd be buying the land," he said. "I hope the owners know that."

"None of them have been back in years. They remember its heyday."

Jack pointed to the rotting porch floor. "Well, if they haven't had recent photos, I'd suggest you take some or I can have my crew take some. If we decide to make an offer, we *all* want to be realistic."

"Of course," she said. "Not sure what your plans are, but I have a client meeting in half an hour. I could call the office and ask one of my associates to take that meeting, if you'd like to grab a drink or dinner?"

"Thanks, but I'd like to get settled in." At her suggestion, he had contacted Mavis LaSalle, who owned a large property east of town that included a spa and event venue. Since wedding season was mostly behind them, one of Mavis's three cottages had been available.

"Oh, that's right, you're out at Mavis's, aren't you?"

"Yup. Looking forward to using the gym and spa."

"Hmm, I wonder if you might be more comfortable in town? I don't know why I didn't suggest the Blueberry B and B. It's charming and right up Beach Road from here. You could stroll down and poke around anytime."

"Thanks, but I'll be fine. I'm not much of a B and B man. Besides, my assistant called ahead and had them stock the cottage with food and drink. I'll be all set."

"Oh well, if you're sure?"

"Absolutely. Shall we?" He gestured toward the driveway. "Don't want you to be late to your meeting."

As Jack turned onto Main Street, he saw the sign for Cove Toys and Games. He checked his watch. Three fifteen. On impulse, he pulled into a space on the street and hopped out. *I feel like a good regional mystery. Let's see if those intriguing ladies are in.*

When he reached the second-floor hall, he faced a wall of doors, none marked until he reached the far end. A small sign for "Merlin's Closet" was on the wall to the left of the door. He knocked and heard a voice call, "Come in!"

A wall of boxes greeted him, no one in sight. "Hello?" he called.

Lolly poked her head around the box wall, said, "Oh!" then disappeared. "Hold on a sec."

Lolly hopped up, vainly endeavoring to smooth her hair. When she emerged, wiping her hands on her jeans, she still had smudges of dust on her nose and cheeks. "We're not... I mean we don't... Lucy's gone home. It's just me here." *Why does this man render me a blithering idiot?*

Jack smiled, stepping around stacks of books as he came closer. "I thought I'd stop in and see if you had a book to recommend."

"Well... It might be tricky. We've been unpacking all day." Lolly felt faint and tongue-tied, novel sensations even after marriage and years of dating before that. *What is it about this stranger?*

"I'm not picky," he said, pulling a handkerchief out of his pocket and leaning forward to touch her nose and cheeks.

Lolly grabbed the handkerchief, furiously wiping her face. "Oh, gee, thanks. I'm sure I look like a fright, covered in dirt."

Like a deer in the headlights. "I think you've got it all."

"Thank you," she said, handing him the dirty handkerchief. "So what kinds of mysteries do you like?"

"Not too fond of cozies. Anything else is fine."

"Hmm... Most of the regionals tend toward the cozy. Do you know

Sally Gunning's work? Her 'water mysteries' are set in a Cape Cod-like area."

"Don't know her, but I'll take one or two. Might you have the first couple in the series?"

"That might take me a few minutes. Feel free to sit, if you can find a place."

Jack leaned against a desk covered with papers and books. *What a perfect round ass*, he thought, watching her move boxes aside, then stoop to search the bottom shelf of a long bookcase. When she stood up and turned, two paperbacks in hand, Lolly knew very well what he'd been doing. Brushing hair from her face, she stepped over book piles, then handed him the books. "Here you go. These should get you started. If you don't like the first, you can always return the second."

"How much do I owe you?"

"Well... I... We don't usually, actually ever sell out of the office. I could... Oh what the heck. Take 'em."

"I couldn't."

"You could. Consider them a welcome-to-town gift." Feeling wobbly and strangely heated, Lolly leaned on a stack of boxes. Before she knew it, the stack tilted, taking her with it.

Jack grabbed her arm with one hand, the other reaching around to catch the topmost box before the pile toppled. "Whoa, Nellybelle."

Before she knew it, they were pressed against each other, Jack fighting to keep them upright. He smelled of spices and the sea, his strong chest crushing her breasts. Breathless, Lolly wondered if she might faint or swoon. Inwardly shaking herself, she thought, *Get a grip, girl! If this is what a man does to you, you've got to get out there and start dating again.* Suddenly, she laughed. "Nellybelle?"

"Might be an obscure term to you. You don't look old enough to remember Roy Rogers. Before my time too. Just slipped out in the heat of the moment."

Heat, you've got that right, she thought. "With the last name Rogers, my Dad was obsessed with that old show. Had us watching it with him all the time growing up."

Finally, he let her go, sorry to lose the warmth and heat. "Hey, how about I buy you a drink to pay for the books? Is there a place nearby?"

"Thanks, I'd love to, but I've got to pick up my daughter. Oh gee, look at the time. Gotta go."

"Another time, then?"

Too tongue-tied to speak, she nodded, grabbing her bag.

They walked out together. "Can I walk you to your car?" he asked.

"Where are you parked?"

He pointed to his SUV. "Just there."

"Well, you go on. I'm up the street. See ya!"

Lolly turned and jogged up the street to the lot alongside Averill's Store. *What is the matter with you?* she thought. *You didn't ask where he's staying, what he's doing here, or how long he'll be around! Stupid, stupid, stupid!*

Jack watched her go, realizing that he hadn't asked where she lived, how old her daughter was, her phone number? Nothing. *You're losing your touch, buddy.*

Jack passed the main house, Netherfield Manor, and two other tree-lined lanes on his way through the property to the dirt road with a small sign that read "Laurel Cottage" on the fence rail. Mavis LaSalle had left the cottage open, keys on the kitchen counter. *Perfect,* he thought, gazing around the one-bedroom house nestled among the trees at the end of a long narrow lane. It was exquisitely furnished in muted colors, with comfortable upholstered chairs and sofas, tasteful artwork on the walls, wrought iron lamps, and an antique dining table and chairs.

After setting his suitcases in the bedroom, he decided to explore the grounds before unpacking. There were several paths around the cottage, and he decided to take the eastern one, hoping to catch a glimpse of the shore and river. As he set off across the lawn, he heard voices and laughter. Before he reached the path, a pretty dark-haired child emerged from the woods, chattering to someone behind her. As Jack paused, the girl, who appeared to be about six or seven, squinted and adjusted her glasses, her chocolate-brown eyes wide. "Mommy, there's a man in the field."

Her companion came into view. "What'd you say, baby?"

Lolly Rogers ruffled her daughter's curls, then looked up. "Oh, it's you again!"

Hestor's Way

Mystery

The Ricky Steele Mysteries

Book 1: *Prepped to Kill*

Book 2: *Gadfly*

Book 3: *Lost in Spindle City*

Book 4: *Poof!*

Also, featuring Ricky Steele:

Jigsaw

Roger and Bess Mysteries

Book 1: *A Friend of Silence*

Book 2: *In the Name of Silence*

Book 3: *The Silence of Memory*

Book 4: *Silencing the Pen* (coming in 2021!)

Young Adult Historical Romance

Song of the Spirit

A NOTE FROM THE AUTHOR

I am so happy to bring you Rich and Karen's love story! This marks the fourth of the *Morgan's Fire* books and also previews number five, *Lolly's Wish*—coming in 2020. A contemporary romance series, *Morgan's Fire* follows Helen, Harriet, Lucy, Gail, Pam, Karen, and a host of strong, resilient women—and men—across the country to the New England coastal town of Horseshoe Crab Cove.

Thank you so much for reading *Rich's Dilemma* and once again visiting Horseshoe Crab Cove with me. I love this beautiful *fictional* village and the colorful, vibrant characters who inhabit it. If you like *Rich's Dilemma* and are willing to write an Amazon review, I would be very grateful. If you would like to sign up for future book releases, giveaways, and occasional notices about my books, please visit *http://www.mleeprescott.com/* and sign up for my newsletter, then follow me on BookBub: *https://www.bookbub.com/search/authors? search=M.+Lee+Prescott*. I promise I will not share your address, nor will I flood you with emails. Do visit my site to read more about my books and hear what's next.

Finally, this book has been revised, proofed, and edited many, many times, but my intrepid assistants and I are human, so if you spot a typo, please email me at *mleeprescott@gmail.com,* and I will fix it. If you'd like to know more about my other books, please scroll ahead to the next section.

Warm wishes,

M. Lee

ABOUT THE AUTHOR

M. Lee Prescott is the author of dozens of works of fiction for adults, young adults, and children, among them *Prepped to Kill*, *Gadfly*, *Lost in Spindle City*, and *Poof!* (Ricky Steele Mysteries), *A Friend of Silence*, *In the Name of Silence*, and *The Silence of Memory* (Roger and Bess Mysteries), *Jigsaw*, and *Song of the Spirit*, and her contemporary romance series, *Morgan's Run*. And now there is Morgan's Fire and book four, *Rich's*  *Dilemma!* In addition to her fiction, her nonfiction books are published by Heinemann, and she has written numerous articles in the field of literacy education. Lee is a professor of education at a small New England liberal arts college, where she teaches reading and writing pedagogy. Her current research focuses on mindfulness and connections to literacy. She regularly teaches abroad, most recently in Singapore.

Lee has lived in southern California (love those Laguna nights!), Chapel Hill, North Carolina, and various spots in Massachusetts and Rhode Island. Currently, she resides in Massachusetts on a beautiful river, where she canoes, swims, and watches an incredible variety of wildlife pass by. She is the mother of two grown sons and spends lots of time with them, their beautiful wives, and her beloved grandchildren. When not teaching or writing, Lee's passions revolve around family, yoga (Kripalu is a second home), swimming, sharing mindfulness with children and adults, and walking.

Lee loves to hear from readers. Email her at _mleeprescott@gmail.com_, and visit her website to hear the latest and sign up for her newsletters!

Visit my author website and sign up for my newsletter at
http://www.mleeprescott.com.
Follow me on BookBub _https://www.bookbub.com/search/authors?
search=M.+Lee+Prescott_!

www.ingramcontent.com/pod-product-compliance
Lightning Source LLC
Chambersburg PA
CBHW061205210726
48294CB00006B/1766